Alone in the Spotlight

. . . .

Brandy Cohen

Catalyst Books

ISBN 978-0-9840303-1-6

Acknowledgments

A special "thank you" to my family, friends
and pets who, thanks to their encouragement,
entertainment, and enthusiasm, have me writing
with a smile on my face. Your suggestions and
gentle honesty is very much appreciated. Also, I
would like to express my gratitude to the wonderful
people at Catalyst Books for helping to make my
dreams come true.

XO,

Brandy

Chapter 1 – The Airport

Lexi noticed him immediately. It was hard not to. He practically knocked her over as he was running to get to the airport security line. *Jeesh*, she thought. *Excuse you.* But she could tell that he was not the kind of man who made apologies. His body language was strong and confident and, though she hated to admit it to herself, sexy. Everything about him led her to believe that this guy was a Class-A jerk. That's probably why she was attracted to him.

Lexi had a history of dating bad men. The kind of men who would run up large bills on her credit card. Who would tell her they loved her and then disappear from her life. Or, worse yet, stalk her.

In short, Lexi Lincoln was a maggot magnet.

But after arriving in Atlanta two years ago, she was convinced her luck had changed. Thanks to weekly sessions with her therapist, Lexi pieced together all of her daddy issues, which were apparently the reason she was so messed up when it came to men. Yes, Lexi finally seemed to have her shit together.

She was dating the very stable and handsome Gregory Williams, whose accounting firm, Williams, Vale and Benson, was a well-respected, up-and-coming firm in the highbrow Buckhead neighborhood of Atlanta. He was quite a catch, or so she was told by her women coworkers.

"Ma'am, this driver's license does not match the name on your ticket. Please step aside," the TSA woman instructed her. She was a small, middle-aged lady with an unnatural color of red hair teased into the shape of a helmet. She held out her arm and pointed Lexi to the right where there was a small group of people waiting. Lexi looked at her for an opportunity to explain, but the woman did not return her gaze. Lexi begrudgingly moved to the other line.

Lexi was furious with herself for doing this yet again. She was so used to filling out forms with the name she'd chosen for herself, Lexi, she had completely forgotten that her license still had her birth name, Mary Lincoln, on it. *Mary was bad enough*, Lexi thought. It was the name of virgins and people who had lambs trailing behind them. But Mary Lincoln? Seriously, what had her mother been thinking? Her dad was the complete opposite of "Honest Abe" Lincoln. He was jerky John Lincoln, the two-bit crook who used prison as a classroom to learn how to become an even bigger loser.

As Lexi walked over to the line to join the other suspicious characters who were also awaiting interrogation, she tried to think happy thoughts. In therapy she learned that by controlling her thoughts she could quickly calm herself down. Within a few seconds, Lexi was back to her usual lighthearted self.

Lexi patiently awaited her turn. Just as she was almost to the front of the line, she let out a loud chuckle in response to the singsong accent of the small, Pakistani man who stood in front of her. Lexi knew it was politically incorrect, but she couldn't help herself. The man turned around and glared at her. He evidently had not learned how to think happy thoughts during stressful situations the way she had. Lexi looked back at him and flashed her smile.

No man could resist a smile from Lexi. It was a broad smile, reminiscent of Julia Roberts', and when Lexi was really happy or laughing, it was accompanied by an adorable dimple on her right cheek. In addition, Lexi's teeth gleamed so brightly you could almost expect to see a tiny Zamboni machine driving around inside her mouth creating a freshly-polished skating rink shine.

Lexi was unaware of the power that her smile afforded her, but the results spoke for themselves. Upon seeing her smiling at him, the Pakistani man's scowl instantly softened and he smiled back at Lexi, throwing in a wink for good measure, before returning his attention to the TSA employee who was addressing him.

Finally, it was Lexi's turn.

"May I see your ticket and photo identification, please?" an elderly man with a cropped gray beard asked her in an authoritative tone.

"Here it is," Lexi complied.

"Who is Lexi?" he asked, looking her square in the eyes.

"Well, you see, I never liked the name Mary Lincoln. It makes me sound like a widow, right? Anyway, I always call myself Lexi. I got it off a soap opera. Cool name, don't you think?" Lexi said with a smile. She hoped she could charm him.

"Ma'am, Lexi's a nice name, but unless you can produce some kind of photo ID to prove that you are indeed Lexi, you will not be flying anywhere today."

That's kind of harsh, Lexi thought.

"Oh, wait, I have some more stuff. Here's my Macy's card. See, it says Lexi."

"There's no photo on it. I'm sorry, but you're going to have to step out of line."

"Seriously?" Lexi wasn't used to being turned down, and she was starting to get annoyed. She hadn't counted on such a hold up when she arrived at the airport just forty-five minutes before her flight's departure, and she knew she was running out of time to deal with all of that nonsense.

Lexi spoke honestly. "Look, I go by Lexi everywhere. I simply made a mistake when I was typing it into the computer buying my ticket. I know, I know, I have to go get a legal name change and then change my license. But do you have any idea how much work all of that is? The DMV alone is a whole day."

There was no reaction from the TSA man. He had nowhere else he needed to be and it seemed like he could care less about her predicament.

Lexi frantically went through her wallet and the many pockets in her purse, pulling out every paper, credit card, or official-looking document she could find to show that she really was Lexi. When she saw that wasn't working, Lexi decided to go hard-core and hit the TSA guy with the sympathy approach, a savvy woman's ace-in-the-hole she'd reserve for men who didn't instantly succumb to her wiles.

"Sir, I'm going home to see my mother. She's recovering from heart surgery. If I have to go now to buy another ticket, I'll miss my flight. You see, all of this happened because I was feeling so upset about what happened to her that when I bought this ticket I made a mistake and typed the wrong name. I guess I just wasn't thinking straight on account of all of the crying. Anyway, my mom is really looking forward to me being home in time for dinner tonight. It's her birthday. She'll be heartbroken, in a different way, if I'm not there to celebrate with her."

Thanks to that ridiculous lie, and Lexi's huge, sympathetic brown eyes, the man scribbled some stuff on her ticket and told her to go to the scanning machine.

Whew, she thought. *That was close.*

Lexi put her carry-on bag on top of the silver rollers and guided it onto the conveyor belt. When Lexi stepped out of her brown wedge shoes she lost four inches off her stature. That part Lexi hated. At only five feet four inches tall, every little bit helped.

Feeling like a literal deer caught in headlights, Lexi did as she was instructed and stood still with her hands on top of her head in the shape of antlers. Seven seconds later she emerged from the X-ray box, retrieved her stuff, regained her height, and headed off towards her gate.

Lexi walked over to the row of electronic flight information screens and saw that her flight was already boarding. Damn! The inquisition had taken a long time, but she knew she had to get some M&M's if she were to make it through the flight without her blood sugar dropping. A quick trip to the newsstand was in order. Lexi picked up a magazine about home design while she was there too. She figured it couldn't hurt to keep up with the latest kitchen trends, even though Lexi didn't even have a kitchen of her own.

She'd been renting a room from Simone and Dale Parker, a cute, young couple she had met at the farmer's market two summers earlier. Dale had been laid off at that time so by renting out their spare bedroom, they were able to keep the bank from foreclosing on their home. It was a perfect situation for Lexi, who was trying to keep her address on the down-low to avoid a creepy ex-boyfriend.

"This is the final boarding call for Flight 925 to Los Angeles. All ticketed passengers should proceed immediately to Gate B-26," the announcement proclaimed.

Lexi hightailed it over to her gate and walked onto the plane, still feeling somewhat relaxed. She knew they would wait for her. Her positive attitude afforded her an ease and confidence that was not always warranted. Luckily, there was room in an overhead bin for her carry-on bag. She stowed it and headed for her seat, holding onto her oversized purse and the plastic bag from the newsstand.

"Excuse me, but I think you're in my seat," Lexi said.

"4C?" the man asked.

"Yes, that's mine." Lexi held up her ticket and showed it to him.

"It says 4D," he told her. "You're next to me, in this seat," he said while motioning to the seat next to the window.

"4D, really? Sorry, I guess I glanced at it too fast."

Lexi knew that her up-close vision wasn't very good, but she hadn't any time to go to the optometrist and get new contacts.

The man stood up so Lexi could step across

him to get to her seat. He was tall and thin, but not in a scrawny, skinny kind of way. He was lean and fit, and it was evident that he worked out. His hair was dark, and sharply contrasted with his piercing blue eyes, eyes that had the same effect on women as Lexi's smile did on men. But Lexi hadn't noticed. She was busy trying to stay upright.

"Are you okay?" He grabbed her arm with one hand and her waist with the other to prevent Lexi from tumbling down.

When she felt his strong hands upon her, a surprising chill ran down Lexi's spine. She was suddenly flustered, but tried to keep her cool and whatever shred of dignity she had left.

Ordinarily, he would've been completely unfazed by the event. After all, Lexi, with her choppy short hair full of different shades of blond, brown, and red, was a far cry from the bombshells he was usually seen with. Yet, touching her sparked something inside him too. He dismissed the feeling immediately.

"Again, I'm so sorry. I think my shoe got caught on the strap from your bag. I'm okay. See, I'm sitting now, safe and sound. Are you okay?" Lexi asked him. "Hope I didn't kick you."

"Fine. No problem. I should've pushed my bag all the way under the seat in front of me, like the flight attendants always say. It was my fault," he said kindly. He held out his hand and smiled, "My name's Sebastian."

Lexi shook his hand, looked into his striking

blue eyes, admired his square jaw, and smiled back. "I'm Lexi. Nice to meet you."

It was him. The guy who tried to mow her over in the terminal. With all the planes flying out of the Atlanta airport, how could he wind up seated right next to her? *This must be a sign*, Lexi thought. *And he doesn't seem like an asshole at all. At least not yet.*

Chapter 2 – The Flight Begins

"Ladies and gentlemen, the door to the aircraft has been closed. Please turn off all electronic devices at this time so we can prepare for takeoff. Thank you."

Lexi went to grab her purse, which she stuffed under the seat in front of her, but she couldn't quite reach it. The first class seats had more legroom than her small legs needed. Sebastian watched in amusement as she unbuckled her seatbelt and practically crawled on the floor to get to her bag. Lexi sat back up, buckled her belt and began the hunt for her phone.

"That's a big bag," Sebastian quipped.

"Yeah, and my phone's small," she responded. "Oh, here it is." As Lexi pulled out her phone, a flurry of papers popped out as well. "Damn that TSA man," she mumbled. If it weren't for him, everything wouldn't be such a mess.

Lexi was about to power down her phone when she saw she had two missed calls, both from Greg. So what choice did she have but to give him a quick call to make sure everything was all right?

"Hi, babe. I saw you called. What's up?" she spoke into her phone.

Sebastian looked up at the flight attendant and shook his head in disapproval. The flight attendant smiled back at him and nodded in agreement.

"Yes, I'm going to miss you too. I'll be back in a few days. Don't worry, everything will be fine. You know how excited I am about this. I'll call you to let you know how it's going...Have a good few days yourself. Oh, gotta go. The flight attendant is giving me the evil eye...Okay...Okay. Bye." Lexi smiled at the flight attendant while turning her phone off. She tucked it back inside her purse and then tossed her purse under the seat.

"Important call?" Sebastian asked snidely.

Lexi didn't pick up on Sebastian's sarcastic tone. "Nah. Just my boyfriend. He's kind of protective," she said matter-of-factly. "So, why are you going to LA?"

"I live there," he said. "You?"

"Really? You live in la-la land? What's it like to be around all those kooky movie business people?"

"Well, it's a lot to take, actually. They can be very insincere, but you gotta make a living, right?"

Sebastian was surprised by his candor. But that's the pleasure of speaking with a stranger: you can say whatever you want knowing you never have to see the person again. Besides, there was something about Lexi that put him at ease. Maybe it was how comfortable she was with her own awkwardness. Whatever the cause, at that moment, his usual guardedness seemed to disappear.

"Yeah. That would make me crazy," she replied. "I like it when I know where people stand. It seems like a lot of work and energy's wasted trying to figure out what fake people are really thinking."

"It is. But you get used to it. Soon, you stop trying to decipher what they're saying and just go with the flow. That's the LA way," he explained.

"Go with the flow? I like that. I try to do that too."

Lexi turned her attention to the window next to her. There were airplanes everywhere. Would they ever get off the ground?

"Hello. This is Captain Kellerman. We are third in line for takeoff. Flight attendants, please prepare the cabin for departure."

As the plane rose into the air, Lexi pulled out her M&M's and began to munch. Of course, they were supposed to be for later in the day when she was feeling run down, but after the morning she'd already had, she figured she could use a bit of sugar.

Lexi poured some candy into her hand and turned to Sebastian. "Want some?"

Sebastian felt conflicted. On the one hand, he really did want some M&M's, but on the other hand, how weird would it be to take candy out of this lady's hand, a woman he just met? "No thanks, I'm good," he replied.

"Sure? They're delicious."

"Well, if you insist."

Lexi smiled and dropped a half-dozen or so of the brightly colored circles into his open hand.

"Enjoy."

"Thanks."

The flight attendant stood next to Sebastian and asked if he wanted something to drink. Sebastian looked to Lexi and said, "What would you like?"

"Um. I don't know. Is it too early for a rum and Coke? Do you serve that?"

"That's fine, ma'am. And you sir? What may I get for you?"

"I'll just have a bottle of water. Thanks," he told her.

Lexi felt like an idiot. She had never flown in first class before, but since she heard that the drinks were free, she just figured everyone would be having a cocktail.

"You know what, I think I'll just have some water right now, too. Sorry to change my order," she told the flight attendant.

"It's okay, ma'am."

Lexi hated the way the lady called her "ma'am." She had just turned twenty-six three weeks earlier. Did that really qualify her as a ma'am? She much preferred the designation she was given for the first twenty-five years of her life, "miss."

"Mr. Hawk. I'm sorry to do this. And I never do this. But I'm a HUGE fan of yours. Would you mind signing this napkin for me?" the flight attendant gushed. And then, when Sebastian asked her for her name, she actually blushed. "Thank you so much. Two waters coming right up!"

"No problem," he replied.

"What was that all about?" Lexi asked. "Are you famous?"

The fact that Lexi had no idea who he was pleased Sebastian immensely. It had been a long time since he came across an unaffected stranger. This made Lexi quite appealing. A regular person. What a treat!

"Yeah, I guess so," he said.

"Why? What do you do?"

"I guess you don't watch a lot of TV, do you?"

Lexi became very animated, "Are you kidding? I love TV. I watch every reality show there is, but I must admit I'm kind of over the whole *Survivor* thing. And *Big Brother* was never really my favorite, either. But I live for all the others."

Sebastian started laughing. "Well, thank goodness not everyone is like you!" She looked at him with a bewildered expression. "I'm an actor," he told her. "I'm on a pretty popular show called *Crime Days and Nights.*"

"I think I've heard of that," Lexi said, unaware of how naïve she sounded. "It's been on for a long time, right?"

"Yes, we just wrapped our sixth season."

"Good for you!" Lexi said with a smile. She didn't mean to be condescending. She just really had no idea what a big deal Sebastian Hawk was to every other woman in North America and most of Europe.

"You know what? Now that you say you're an actor, I think I've heard of you. Did the flight attendant say your last name is Hawk? You're Sebastian Hawk! Yes, I know who you are. You were in *People* magazine, right?"

Sebastian smiled. He'd been in countless magazines throughout the years, but what Lexi was probably referring to was last year's issue where he was listed as one of *People*'s sexiest men alive.

"Yeah, I've been in there."

"Okay, okay. I know you. You're like REALLY famous! I'm so sorry I didn't recognize you. Like I said, I don't watch your show. Sorry. Crime stuff isn't my thing."

"It's perfectly fine. What do you do, Lexi?"

"Well, I used to sell soap. Fancy bar soaps to snooty boutiques, but that got a bit boring so I went back to school and became a dental hygienist. I know a lot of people think that's a weird job, sticking your hands inside people's mouths, but I really enjoy it. When my patients leave me they're so happy to have such shiny smiles." Lexi smiled at Sebastian as though to show him exactly what she was talking about.

Just as with all other men, Lexi's smile drew Sebastian in.

"Well, between the soap thing and the teeth cleaning, I would have thought you were a clean freak, but I saw all that stuff fall out of your bag, so I'm guessing that's not necessarily the case," he teased.

"I do like to keep things organized. That whole mess with my papers was entirely the TSA people's fault. They were giving me a really hard time and almost didn't let me through security," she explained defensively.

"Why? Are you a terrorist?" Sebastian joked.

"Yes. You caught me. Call your new flight attendant friend – Patty is it? – and have me arrested right now!" Lexi retorted.

The banter was fun. They both were enjoying themselves and as they chatted, the time ticked by. Sebastian hadn't had such a frank, relaxed conversation in a very long time. Talking with Lexi reminded him of how he acted before he *acted* – when he was just a regular, nice guy and not a famous celebrity. It felt good to revisit that part of himself.

Soon, it was mealtime and Patty was back.

"Mr. Hawk, we have a special meal for you. I'll have it brought right over, but first I wanted to offer you another beverage. Perhaps a glass of wine or champagne?" She fawned all over him.

"Sure, a glass of red wine would be nice."

"And you, ma'am?" Patty asked Lexi.

"White wine, please."

Lexi turned to Sebastian. "You get a special meal? Wow, being an actor has its perks."

"I always order vegetarian meals because I'm a bit leery of the mystery meats they serve on airplanes."

"Even in first class? I thought the food up here's supposed to be better than the crap they try to sell you in coach."

"I hope this doesn't make me sound like a jerk, but it's been so long since I've flown coach that I didn't know they charged extra for meals there," Sebastian confessed.

"Oh yeah. It costs like fifteen dollars for a lame turkey sandwich."

"Really? That's ridiculous."

"Yup, sure is."

Patty laid a napkin on Lexi's tray table and then handed Lexi her tray of food. There was chicken, a salad, a roll, and dessert. Lexi thought it all looked delicious. It'd been well over an hour since she'd downed her M&M's and she was feeling pretty hungry.

Patty then carefully placed Sebastian's plate of roasted vegetables upon his napkin-covered tray table. "I hope you enjoy this, Mr. Hawk. Let me know if I can get you anything." Patty smiled as she spoke.

"Okay, thanks," he said without paying her much attention. He was fascinated by Lexi and was watching her intently.

Patty walked away feeling dejected.

Lexi ate almost everything she was given, including the roll and the raspberry cheesecake. Sebastian couldn't recall the last time he witnessed a woman eating so much. In LA, everyone was on a diet. He discretely looked Lexi up and down and found her body to be pretty hot. Sebastian smiled to himself.

"How's your food?" Lexi asked him.

"It's okay," he responded. "I can see you really enjoyed yours."

"I did. The chicken tasted fine. You don't have to be afraid of it," she said, trying to comfort him.

"I'm not afraid of it, I...I...I just don't like to be surprised by things," Sebastian tried to explain. "Once, several years ago, I got sick on an airplane and I'm pretty sure it was because of the food."

"So that was enough for you to throw in the towel on airplane food for the rest of your life?"

"Well no, I'm eating the vegetables they gave me, aren't I?" When Sebastian heard the words come out of Lexi's mouth it made him sound like a wuss. He vowed to himself to order a steak on his next flight and take whatever happened to him like a man. When had he become so fussy? So Hollywood?

"I'm not a quitter," he insisted.

"Okay, sorry. I didn't mean to insult you. I was just wondering. I guess you learn faster than me, that's all. It takes me a lot of times of getting hurt before I give up on something."

"Something or someone? It sounds like you're talking about more than airplane food."

Sebastian's instincts were right, of course. Lexi's comment stemmed from the many times she was, in her opinion, summarily dumped, as well as from her own inabilities to leave bad relationships in a timely manner. She would often stay in them until they became downright toxic.

"Okay, you caught me. I have a thing about people, well, I guess if I'm being honest, it's especially about men, who jump from person to person because of what they deem to be a flaw. I think it's the flaws that make each of us special," Lexi said emphatically.

"Yes, we men do tend to have A.D.D. when it comes to women."

"A.D.D.? Do you mean Attention Deficit Disorder or After Double D's?" She looked at Sebastian and rolled her eyes. "You men seem to all want the same thing, and then when you get it, you want something else. What's up with that?"

Sebastian was taken aback. No one had spoken to him like that...ever. Sure he liked big breasts, but this wasn't about him, was it? She was attacking all men and he had to stand up for his kind.

"You women aren't any better, I can tell you that from experience. You think men have no feelings at all. You use us for our bank accounts and then jump into bed with our close friends the first chance you get."

This was getting personal. Lexi knew Sebastian must have been hurt pretty badly to be so sensitive to her remark. She tried to tread lightly, but that had never been her specialty.

"So your girlfriend slept with your friend?" she asked. "That's horrible. I'm so sorry."

She was sorry, but at the same time it made Lexi feel good to know that even gorgeous, famous actors who got special treatment had trouble when it came to love. Of course, that shouldn't be a surprise to someone who reads *People* magazine. Lexi was usually pretty good at keeping up with the latest Hollywood break-ups, but she didn't recall reading about Sebastian's.

"It's okay. It's just a little fresh, that's all. I'd been dating another actress, Amanda, for the last several months and I just went down to St. Thomas to surprise her, only I was the one who got surprised. I found her with Tom, who's been my personal assistant and friend for years. Apparently he was more interested in assisting her than me, if you know what I mean."

"You were just there? Today?"

"Yeah, I found them together last night when I arrived, so I caught the first flight out and here I am, enjoying your lovely company. How about if we have some stronger drinks now? Do you feel like having some vodka with me?"

Lexi was stunned. Poor man.

"That's a nightmare. I've been where you are, Sebastian, I can tell you. But he wasn't with an old friend of mine, more like with my nemesis. So it was only a single betrayal, not a double like you just had. Can I give you a hug?"

Lexi didn't wait for his response. She leaned over to him, with the seatbelt still wrapped around her waist, and grabbed Sebastian around his neck. "It'll be okay," she whispered in his ear.

Sebastian hugged her back. He really needed it more than he realized. Who was this angel? He held her tight. It was all he could do to let Lexi go but he was afraid if he didn't, he might start crying. That would be terrible. Not only was he a man, but he was famous for God's sake. He had a reputation to uphold.

"Thanks. How about those drinks?" he said when Lexi finally released him.

"Works for me."

Sebastian summoned Patty over and in a moment they both had vodka on the rocks.

"Bottoms up!" Sebastian said as they clinked glasses.

Chapter 3 – The Drinks

Lexi never drank vodka straight-up before and she thought it tasted like lighter fluid. She had Patty bring her some orange juice, which she promptly mixed into her glass. *Ah, a screwdriver, much better*, she thought.

Sebastian inhaled his first glass in no time flat. He could no longer avoid the feelings of hurt and heartache that he had been trying so desperately to ignore. Drowning them seemed to be the logical solution.

Lexi and Sebastian talked and talked as they drank and drank. Soon, they were both quite inebriated and their conversation reflected it.

"What's up with your crazy hair?" Sebastian asked Lexi.

"Hey! What do you mean crazy? I like my hair, thank you very much," Lexi said, smiling at Sebastian while running her hands through her many layers.

Sebastian joined in on the fun. He unbuckled his seat belt so he could face Lexi and then started playing with her hair. "This piece right here. What color is this one? Orange?"

Lexi laughed. "Shut up, you jerk. It's a woman's prerogative to change her mind, so what if I can't decide on a hair color?"

"Wait, wait, I think this one's my favorite. It's like four colors on one strand. Fantastic!" he said animatedly.

They both laughed. Normally, a comment like that would have qualified Sebastian as an asshole, but whether it was the vodka or his charming, flirtatious manner, Lexi was not offended at all.

"And let's look at your hair, Mr. Bigshot," she challenged him.

"What's wrong with MY hair?"

"It's black, like a vampire's," she laughed.

"They make me dye it that color for the show."

"You're kidding!" Lexi became hysterical.

"It's really light brown." As he said it, Sebastian broke up, too. They were both laughing so hard they could barely breathe, and Patty kept bringing them more liquor.

Finally, Patty brought some snacks.

"I want the cookies and the candy bar," Lexi said, as she reached across Sebastian to pull the goodies out of Patty's basket.

"Chips for me," Sebastian said. When Patty handed Sebastian his small bag of potato chips she gently touched his arm, but he didn't notice her overtures. He was having so much fun with Lexi that no one else seemed to exist.

Out of the blue, Sebastian lifted up Lexi's blouse. "Where do you put it all?" he innocently asked, checking out her flat stomach.

Lexi pushed his hand and her shirt down as fast as she could. She was in shock from the incident, but couldn't stop from laughing. "Cut it out. You're going to get us in trouble," she told him.

"With who, Patty? I think we can handle her. Besides, I want to know how you have such a slamming body when you eat so much. What's your secret?"

"I do kickboxing. And sometimes I run. What about you?" Lexi pulled Sebastian's shirt up, revealing his stomach. It was tight and sexy. She knew it would be, but she had to see it for herself and this seemed like the perfect opportunity, all in good fun.

"Hey, I pay the finest trainers in the world to make sure I look this way," he said, a little arrogantly.

"Well, I think you should ask for a refund," Lexi teased.

Sebastian held up his own shirt and looked at his stomach. He saw a six pack. "Really? You're not impressed, huh?"

Lexi rubbed her hand across Sebastian's stomach and said, "Nah, my dog has better abs."

Of course, Lexi didn't have a dog, but that wasn't the point.

"Well, I'm sorry to disappoint you. Perhaps I should hire Rover's trainer. What's his name? I'll put it in my phone."

"It's me, you ass. And I bet if you worked out with me, you could eat all the candy you wanted, too!"

Sebastian looked at Lexi. He was so attracted to her that her proposition sounded perfect to him. They say when you fall off a horse you should get right back on and, since he had just been dumped, why not rebound with the hot girl in the seat next to him?

"What did you have in mind? Do you want to go in the bathroom with me? A mile-high club kind of thing?"

Lexi could hear a change in Sebastian's tone. He was serious.

"No, I was just joking. Jeesh, calm down. I thought we were having fun," she told him.

"We are having fun. I just thought of a way we could have some more fun. Plus, you could help me burn off these calorie-laden chips I'm about to eat."

"Ha, ha! Not gonna happen."

"Why not?" Sebastian asked, blinking his blue eyes at her.

Looking at his stunning face made Lexi want to jump him right there in the seat, but she had self-control...and a boyfriend.

"Greg."

"Who?"

"My boyfriend. I have a boyfriend. His name's Greg and he's a good guy. Some people are loyal."

Lexi heard the words come out of her mouth and instantly felt bad.

"Yeah, I forgot that some women are decent," he replied, dropping his head down.

"I'm so sorry, Sebastian. I shouldn't have said that considering what you're going through. Come on, let's change the subject."

"No," he replied. "You know what? I think I'm just going to close my eyes and sleep right now. Two rejections in less than twenty-four hours is more than a guy's ego can take."

"That's not fair. I'm not rejecting you. Under any other circumstances I would be in that bathroom humping you," she said smiling, trying to cheer him up. "It's just that I finally have a good guy in my life and I don't want to do anything to mess that up. Some day you'll have a good woman in your life, too. Really."

Lexi stroked his arm.

Sebastian felt sad. He turned to Lexi and kissed her on her cheek. "Thanks."

A couple of moments of quiet passed and then Lexi said, "Oh, what the hell!"

She couldn't deny their strong chemistry. Lexi unbuckled her seatbelt, fumbled around so she could stand up in front of Sebastian, bent over him putting her hands on his broad shoulders and began kissing him on his lips. It was a bold move, but Lexi was like that, especially when she had a few drinks in her.

Sparks flew. The kiss lasted forever and finally Lexi plopped back down into her seat. Sebastian's male hormones were raging. The alcohol fueled both their passions. He lifted the armrest that separated them, put his arms around her back and pulled her towards him while he leaned in. They started making out, big time, in row 4.

The other passengers didn't seem to notice. They wore headphones and were engrossed by their movies or laptops. As Sebastian's left hand traveled up the inside of Lexi's blouse, her hands found their way to his pants. Their kissing was wet and sloppy, much like the way a little kid eats a melting ice cream cone. Tongues were everywhere until Sebastian got a firm tap on his shoulder. He reluctantly pulled away from Lexi and looked up.

"Hi Patty," he said.

Patty had a serious expression on her face. "Mr. Hawk, we're going to be landing soon. The captain has turned on the fasten seat belt sign and requested that all passengers prepare for arrival," she said in a disapproving tone.

"Oh, already? Okay. Thanks."

Lexi should've been embarrassed, but she didn't embarrass easily. Besides, she was still super drunk.

"You have to put your seatbelt on," Sebastian told Lexi.

"You do it for me," she said coyly.

Sebastian secured his seatbelt and then began kissing Lexi again, this time on her neck. She squealed a little while his hands moved around her waist and under her bottom feeling for her seatbelt. When he found both ends, he clicked them together and then they giggled.

"Okay, I guess we have to behave now," Lexi said.

"You're incredible," Sebastian told her. "How long are you going to be in LA?"

"Three days. Why, what did you have in mind?" she said flirtatiously.

"Nothing. Nothing at all. Just taking a visitor's census," he teased.

"Good, because I'm going to be quite busy while I'm there. I won a contest, did I mention that?"

"Really? For what? Your cuteness?" Sebastian smiled at Lexi.

Lexi pushed Sebastian's shoulder, like they were a couple of fifteen-year-olds flirting in math class. "No, for selling tons of teeth-whitening products."

Sebastian started laughing. "That's so hot!"

"Shut up! I realize I don't get to pretend to be a detective for a living, but people need white teeth, too. Especially in your business, am I right?"

"Yup. A white smile does go a long way out in, as you call it, la-la land. And I don't pretend to be a detective, by the way. I have researched the role and use my extensive performance skills to create a realistic portrayal."

"I'm so sorry, Mr. Fake Detective. I'm sure you're a regular Sherlock Holmes," she patronized him.

The wheels of the plane touched down and the flight was over.

Chapter 4 – The Arrival

Patty watched as Sebastian got Lexi's carry-on bag down from the overhead compartment and then as the two of them exited the plane together. They walked through the terminal chatting about nonsense until they approached the airport's exit where Lexi turned to Sebastian and held out her arm to shake his hand. "Thanks for making the flight go by so fast. It was great meeting you," she said.

"What? That's it? You were just using me?" Sebastian said in a kidding manner. "How 'bout if I give you a ride to your hotel. You're staying in Marina Del Rey, right? That's on my way. I could have my driver drop you there, no problem."

"That's a nice offer, Sebastian, but see that man over there with the sign that says 'Lincoln', that's me. He's here to drive me to my hotel."

"So what? Let me take you. Besides, aren't you

hungry for some dinner? My treat! I gotta tell you, those veggies and chips didn't quite fill me up."

"Hey, don't forget about the M&M's I gave you."

"Oh yeah. Well, now I feel full!"

"Okay. Take me to my hotel so I can freshen up and then we can grab some dinner. That actually sounds quite nice. Thanks."

Lexi walked over to the driver who was holding the sign with her name on it and told him thanks for coming, but she had an alternate means of transportation.

Sebastian turned to Lexi and said, "Just one more thing. I'm sorry about this, but there are probably going to be paparazzi outside this terminal. Would you mind if we walked out separately? They think I'm still with Amanda and I don't want to start rumors." He looked through the airport's glass doors and pointed at some parked cars. "Mine's the black one over there, by the red truck. The driver's name is Sam. I'll call him and tell him you're coming first. Do you mind?"

"Wow, that's pretty strange. But then again, I'm actually kind of used to sneaking around. It's a long story I'll bore you with another time. No problem. I get it," she agreed.

"Thanks. See you in a few minutes." Sebastian smiled. As Lexi walked away from him, he put on a pair of dark sunglasses.

Lexi found Sam who was just hanging up the phone from Sebastian when she walked up to the car. "This way, miss," he said while opening a door for her.

Lexi liked Sam. He called her miss.

Sebastian was right about the paparazzi. They snapped pictures of him just walking to his car. *How dumb*, Lexi thought.

As they drove on the freeway, Sebastian cozied up to Lexi. She found it sweet, the way he snuggled into her shoulder. She put her leg on top of his and they held hands, but no words were spoken until they arrived at Lexi's hotel a few minutes later.

"Thanks, Sam," Sebastian said. "Please hang on to my bag. I'll call you later."

"My pleasure, sir," Sam responded.

Lexi went up to the reception desk and checked in. There was a gift bag waiting for her from Dental Dream Whitening, the company that sponsored the contest. She took the colored gift bag and her room key and met up with Sebastian who was hiding out by the elevators with her suitcase.

"Room 623," she announced to him once they got into the elevator.

"That's my lucky number," Sebastian joked.

As soon as they were inside her room, Lexi explored her gift bag. She loved surprises, especially ones that included sweets like this one did.

"So a dental products company gives you sugary stuff as a welcome gift? Kind of self-serving, don't you think? You eat all that crap, your teeth start rotting and then you need more of their products," Sebastian said shaking his head.

"Hey, don't knock it or I won't give you any."

"Okay, what's in there? Any Oreos?"

"Ha! For a health nut actor, you sure do have a sweet tooth," Lexi commented.

"Who said I'm a health nut? And I wasn't always an actor, you know. I used to be a waiter!" They laughed. "Actually, I was never a waiter because I can't balance lots of plates at once. But, I did deliver pizzas for a little while when I was in college, so that's sort of like being a waiter."

"Where'd you go to college?" Lexi asked.

"UCLA. I wanted to be a computer programmer. Sexy right? I was really into I.T. before the acting bug hit me."

"You're a computer geek? Interesting. I bet you'd have made a great dentist!" Lexi said encouragingly.

Sebastian ignored the dentist comment. "All this talk about food has made me hungry. How about we get some real food now? Wanna order room service?" Sebastian suggested.

"Room service? Why don't we go to a restaurant?" she asked.

"I'm sorry, but it's that paparazzi thing again. Once word breaks about my split it won't be such a big deal, but right now I'd love to keep it quiet, if you don't mind."

Lexi was tired from the flight and the vodka so the idea of staying in worked for her. Sebastian found the room service menu on the desk, which was next to the dresser, across from the bed. He

read off the selections and they decided to split
the salmon with dill and the filet mignon. Surf and
turf, as Lexi called it.

Even though they had just spent several hours
together, telling each other things they didn't dare
share with any of their friends, there was still an
awkwardness between them as they waited for
their food to arrive. Sebastian realized that they
were drunk for most of the flight so he figured it
made sense to hit the mini bar.

"Yes, here it is. Would you like some more
vodka?" Sebastian asked. "Or, if you prefer, I can
fix you that rum and Coke you ordered when we
first got on the plane."

Lexi was surprised he remembered what she
liked to drink and it pleased her that he paid
attention.

"Rum and Coke would be great, thanks."

Sebastian mixed Lexi's drink, handed it to her
and then took her other hand and walked with
her over to the bed. It was a pretty, fluffy bed with
white linens and several white pillows carefully
placed across the headboard. They sat down on the
edge of it and began to kiss. At that moment, the
worst possible time of course, Lexi's phone rang.
She got up to answer it.

"Hi, Greg. What's up? Don't worry about me.
Everything's fine. The flight was good and I'm just
about to have some dinner. How about you? What
have you been up to today?...Ahuh...Yeah...Um.
Good. Glad to hear it. It's about time they came

around. Okay, better run now. Have a good night... Thanks, you too. Talk to you tomorrow. Bye."

"That was weird," Sebastian remarked.

"Weird for you? Imagine how I feel."

Lexi was never a cheater. It was something she detested about men, although she found herself in the very situation she would have condemned anyone else for. Yet Lexi simply couldn't help herself because she felt a very strong connection to Sebastian.

"Do you mind if I ask how long you've been with him? I mean, that wasn't exactly the warmest conversation and you're such a passionate girl. I'm just kind of surprised by the coolness of it all."

"I've known Greg for like a year now, but we've only been dating a couple of months. He's a very proper guy. It's not that Greg's not passionate, he's just kind of, well, to be frank, got a bit of a stick up his ass!" Lexi laughed. "Sorry, I know that's rude. He treats me very nicely and he's wonderful, really, but when I'm drunk I tend to be a bit too honest."

"Oh, yeah? What do you think about me, then? Now that you have all that truth serum in your system?"

Sebastian put on his sweetest face. As an actor, he was quite adept at altering his expression as needed. Truth be told though, he was a bit nervous awaiting her response. Lexi was far more forthright than anyone he'd ever met. Like most artists, his ego was somewhat fragile, and even more so that night, after just being dumped.

"Well, you're pretty damn cute, that's for sure. As for whether or not you're a good guy, the jury's still out. Did you know that you practically knocked me over in the Atlanta airport when you were running to security?"

"I did? I had no idea. I'm so sorry."

"Yes, you did. And you never said 'excuse me.' I think you have the potential to be a real asshole!" she teased. "But, you also have the potential to be a ton of fun. Let's see how it goes, okay?"

"Let me show you how much fun I can be," Sebastian said with a charming smile. He stood up and once again took Lexi's hand, leading her over to the bed.

"Is sex the only thing you think about?"

"Um, right now, yeah. Aren't you thinking about it?" he asked as they both sat on the edge of the bed.

Lexi was conflicted. Even though every ounce of her body was pulling her to sleep with Sebastian, her mind told her she needed to be faithful to Greg. She stood up. "I'm going to unpack and freshen up. How about you? Do you want to brush your teeth or something?"

"Do I have bad breath?" Sebastian put his cupped hand in front of his mouth and blew into it. All he could smell was vodka, which he thought smelled pretty good.

"Oh, I forgot. It's the dental hygienist in you. How many times a day do you floss?" he teased.

Lexi ignored him and went into the bathroom

to brush, yes, but also to fix her hair and reapply some make-up. *There, not bad*, she thought.

It wasn't long before room service arrived and it smelled delicious. They took the cart over to the table and chairs that were next to the window. The brown velvet drapes were shut, but it was still a nice setting.

"I must admit, this is pretty romantic," Lexi said quietly. She took a large bite of salmon, another sip of her drink and then guided her foot up toward Sebastian's thigh.

"If you're going to do that, I can't eat."

"Okay, you're right. Let's eat. I'm starving," Lexi agreed.

"So, what's that story you promised to bore me with about you sneaking around? Have you been a baaad girl?" Sebastian smirked.

"God, you hear everything, don't you?"

"It's my job. I pay attention to details. Like your hair. I noticed that you fixed it differently when you were in the bathroom a few minutes ago. It's less fluffy now, but I like it any way you wear it," he told her.

When Sebastian first met Lexi he thought her hair was off-putting, but that was when he was still behaving like an elitist celebrity. Now, after being affected by Lexi's realness, he was feeling and acting more like his truer, nicer self. He came to think of her hair as adorable, just like her.

"Thanks for the compliment on my hair," Lexi said as she stroked the top of her head. "It's in transition. I kind of think everything in life is about transitions, don't you? I mean we're never done doing anything until we're dead, and then who cares, right? I feel like each and every day I experience something new, and that helps me grow as a person."

"Wow, that's a lot to take in on all this booze," Sebastian admitted. "But yeah, I guess I agree. I'm just not sure it's all growth. Sometimes we have setbacks and that's all they are."

"That's the tricky part. You think they're setbacks at first, but they really help us learn something that will benefit us in the future," Lexi said. Then she thought for a moment and added, "Or, maybe you're right, they're just problems that plague us. I'll concede that point."

"Are you going to tell me your sneaking around story or not?" Sebastian pushed. He wanted the dirty details.

"You know, I wonder if this is something we have in common. A couple of years ago I had a stalker. Did you ever have one of those?" she asked.

"No, can't say I have, though I do have women chase me down the streets sometimes."

"Why? Do you steal ladies' purses?" Lexi laughed.

"That's it! Where's yours? Bet you can't find it because I've tucked it into my back pocket – though your purse is huge so I guess I would need some serious cargo pants if that were to be true."

He smiled.

"Ha, ha. Well, my stalker experience was not quite so funny. His name's Travis Orrington and we used to go out."

Sebastian looked puzzled. "You dated your stalker?"

"No you idiot, I dated Travis and when we broke up he started stalking me. He couldn't accept that I didn't want to be with him," she explained.

"Why'd you break up with him?"

"Because he was insane, which is not something I noticed until our third date. That's when the lunatic Travis came out. When I gave him the 'let's be friends' speech, he went nuts, right there in the Red Lobster. He stood up and yelled at me saying that I was the one who was crazy. He said he was perfect for me and if I wasn't smart enough to see it yet, then he'd find ways to prove to me that I'm wrong."

"Holy shit. Were you scared? What'd he do?"

"I wasn't scared at first, just kind of pissed. How dare he imply that I was crazy? It wasn't until the notes started appearing everywhere that I began to get scared," she said.

"Notes?"

"Yeah, lots of them. That's when I dubbed him 'The Leech'. He would send me fifty e-mails a day, write all over my Facebook wall, tape them to the door of my apartment and the windshield of my car. He even managed to put some on my office desk without anyone at work noticing him.

"What'd the notes say?" Sebastian was riveted.

"They said all kinds of things. Some were romantic, about how he would take me to the beach at night so we could enjoy the stars. And others were threatening, like the one that said he wanted to cut off my hands to keep them for himself."

"That's scary as shit!"

"I know. I cried when that one arrived. I took it to the police and got a restraining order against him, but Travis still didn't stop. That's when I moved to Atlanta," she explained.

"Wait. Are you telling me that this guy kept threatening you and no one could do anything about it? Your only option was to recreate your life in another city?" Sebastian was shocked.

"Yeah, that about sums it up. Since I've been in Atlanta, I changed all of my numbers, e-mail addresses, Internet usernames, everything. Oh, by the way, my real name is Mary. Nice to meet you."

"Mary? It's like you're in the witness protection program."

"Uhuh, but without the protection. And since I've been with Greg, my life's been calm. So you see, excitement and passion can be overrated."

"It sounds like one of the story lines from my TV show, except it's real and it happened to you. You poor thing. Come here."

Sebastian stood up and motioned to Lexi to do the same. He pulled her into him and gave her a firm embrace. At six foot one, Sebastian towered over Lexi, whose head reached just beyond his shoulder, and that was with her shoes on. They hugged for a few moments before Lexi exhaled and began to cry.

"I'm sorry, but I haven't talked about The Leech in a long time," she said in between bouts of sobs. "I've tried to put that part of my life behind me, but every time I look at my old name on my driver's license, like I did at the airport, it reminds me that my life's a lie."

Sebastian squeezed her even tighter and rubbed her back. "It's okay, Lexi, or should I call you Mary?"

"Lexi," she said, tears streaming down her face.

Sebastian was an only child so consoling others was not something he was accustomed to doing. Plus, as a celebrity, people usually tiptoed around his feelings. This was out of his comfort zone, but he tried his best to make Lexi feel better.

"You know, my life's a lie too," he said a few moments later. "My real name's Harvey, Harvey Braxton."

Lexi looked up at Sebastian and wiped her tears. "Huh?"

He looked down at her with his arms still wrapped around her waist and said, "Harvey's not exactly a movie star name, is it? Not that I'm a movie star, well, at least not yet. My agent told me to change it when I moved here ten years ago. My parent's still haven't forgiven me."

Lexi smiled. "Thanks for that. You cheered me up." She rubbed her wet hands on Sebastian's sleeve. He didn't mind.

"You know, Lexi, I've had a bad run with women too, though I would never compare my problems to what you've been through. But still, I can't understand how Amanda could have cheated on me. I was really looking forward to surprising her on vacation because it's not often when we're both on breaks from our shows. Serves me right, I guess. Surprises never seem to work out for me."

Lexi looked up at Sebastian. "That sucks. She's an idiot. You deserve better."

Maybe it was because of all the alcohol or maybe it was just because he and Lexi were sharing such an honest, tender moment, but right then Sebastian began to quietly cry. Lexi now pulled him into her. He put his head down on her shoulder and let the waterworks flow.

"What a pair we are," Lexi said. Then she started crying again. The two of them stood next to the table by the window hugging and crying. Before long, they made their way over to the bed, kicked off their shoes and lay down, still holding each other tightly. Sex was the furthest thing from either of their minds. And then they fell asleep.

Chapter 5 – The Next Morning

Lexi awoke at 6:30 a.m., which was really 9:30 a.m. for her since her body was still on Eastern time. It was a long sleep and she felt great, except for the massive headache that was coming on strong. Undoubtedly a side effect of her alcoholic excesses from the day before. She looked over at Sebastian who was sleeping in his clothes and thought he looked like an innocent little boy. *So sweet – and yet so hot!*

She tiptoed over to her things, gathered what she needed, and schlepped all of it into the bathroom with her. Her first order of business was to pop a couple of Motrin. The headache was pulsating through her eyes. Then she looked up into the mirror. Lexi was horrified by what she saw. It was a monster morning! Lexi hadn't had one of those in a long time. There was makeup smeared all over her face, creating a particularly

unappealing design of black and pink streaks
on her cheeks. Downright frightening! Thank
goodness Sebastian was still asleep. She attacked
her skin with make-up remover and then got
into the shower for a more intense and thorough
scrubbing.

Sebastian awoke to the *Crime Days and Nights*
theme song. It was his ringtone. He looked around
to try and figure out where he was and then it
dawned on him. He looked at the clock. Shit! It
wasn't even 7:00 a.m. Who could be calling him at
that ungodly hour? He pulled the phone out of his
pants pocket, but the person had already hung up.
He checked to see if there was a message and sure
enough, there was. It was from Matt, his publicist.
What could be so important? Sebastian didn't
bother to listen to the message. Instead he just
pushed the button to return the call.

"Matt, do you know what time it is? What's up,
man?" he spoke in a crackly, morning voice.

"Where the hell are you, Sebastian?"

"Why?"

"Why? Because you're in the middle of a crisis!"
Matt's voice became very loud and it irritated
Sebastian's head, which was pounding.

"Calm down, man. My head's killing me. What
the hell are you talking about? Did someone die?
Are my parents okay?"

"Yeah, yeah, your family's fine. No one's
dead, except maybe your reputation!" Matt said
animatedly.

"I don't understand. Maybe because it's so freaking early! Please slow down and tell me exactly what you're trying to say," Sebastian insisted calmly.

"Sebastian, it's all over the Internet. You cheated on Amanda by having sex with some girl on an airplane. What the fuck's up with that?" Matt asked.

"WHAT!!!" Sebastian was startled and had to regroup for a moment. "First of all, Amanda was the one cheating on me with Tom, yes, Tom, my now former friend-slash-assistant. I found them on top of each other in St. Thomas when I went down there to surprise her."

"Oh shit. Sorry, man. So, how come there's photos and even a video of you and a girl having sex on an airplane?"

"That's insane. I didn't have sex with her. We had too many drinks and we kissed a little. THAT'S ALL. It was nothing. How is there even footage of it?" Sebastian was confused. He was also unaware that Lexi was in the bathroom drying off from her shower and applying her make-up. She could hear every word he was saying.

"I don't know, but it's out there. Who is she? An actress?" Matt asked.

"She's nobody. Just some chick in the seat next to me. My rebound girl, that's it."

"Well, it looks like the two of you were fucking. I have some serious damage control to do. Where are you now?" Matt sounded frantic.

"I'm in her hotel, but nothing happened, really. You gotta believe me, man," Sebastian pleaded.

"I believe you, but it doesn't look good. Get the hell out of there right away," Matt insisted.

"Okay, yeah, I will."

"And be discrete for God's sake. Call me when you're home."

"Yeah, man. Thanks. Bye." Sebastian hung up with Matt and immediately placed another call.

"Sam? Sorry to call you so early, but can you come to the hotel you dropped me off at yesterday? Oh, and pick me up in the side alley. Thanks, see you in ten."

When Lexi heard Sebastian finish his calls, she stormed out of the bathroom. She looked beautiful, even angelic, with her wet hair and flowy, colorful sundress.

"You ARE an asshole!" she screamed at Sebastian.

"What?" Sebastian tried to look innocent. He raised both of his hands to the sides of his head. It hurt so bad that he thought if he didn't hold onto it, it could actually explode.

"Good morning, Lexi," he said sweetly.

"Good morning, my ass, you scumbag! I'm a nobody, huh? Just some rebound chick? Well screw you! Get out of here right now!" she yelled while throwing his shoes at him.

Sebastian ducked and then looked back up at her. "Lexi, did you hear my conversation? I'm so sorry, but let me explain, please."

"You've got one minute...go!" she said while looking at the clock on the nightstand.

"Come on Lexi, you had to know I didn't mean that."

"Forty-five seconds."

"Okay, here it is. That was my publicist, Matt. Apparently someone took pictures and video of us having some fun on the plane yesterday and posted them on the Internet. It makes us look like we're having sex and what's even worse, for me anyway, is that now everyone thinks I'm the one cheating on Amanda," Sebastian explained.

"Ten seconds."

"Come on. I have a splitting headache and I didn't know what to say to my publicist. He thought you were an actress. I just said, no, you're not an actress, that's all. That's what I meant by 'you're nobody'...You're nobody famous. Of course you're somebody! You're somebody very special."

Sebastian stood up and approached Lexi. "Please, please forgive me." He sounded quite sincere and apologetic. "By the way, you look gorgeous this morning." And then he kissed her cheek.

"Yeah, well you look like shit, but I'll give you another chance. Like I said, I don't quit on something because it hurts me once, but the second time I get hurt, so do you. I mean it! I throw a strong right hook," Lexi said with a bit of a smirk.

How could she stay mad at such a cute face?

Besides, what he said made sense. She knew how much he was hurting over Amanda's betrayal and she felt kind of bad that now he had to face more problems because of the internet stuff. His life really sucked.

Sebastian walked over to Lexi and hugged her. "You really are special," he told her warmly. "I'm so sorry, but I have to go and try to fix this mess. My publicist is having an aneurism. Is that okay?"

"Do whatever you have to do. I'm going on a special tour of Universal Studios today with the other contest winners."

"That sounds like fun," he replied.

Lexi tried to play it cool. Sebastian went to the bathroom, cleaned himself up and then kissed Lexi properly, sensually.

"I'll call you later. I promise," he said. Then he walked out the door wearing his sunglasses. *Some disguise*, Lexi laughed to herself.

It was a good thing she had a stable guy like Greg, she thought. *There's none of that ridiculousness with him. He's just a good guy. A little dull perhaps, but good.* As far as Lexi was concerned at that moment, good was great.

Lexi went down to the lobby and enjoyed a hot breakfast. It was so satisfying, especially since she really didn't eat much dinner and the booze was still swirling around in her stomach. While she was sipping her coffee, her phone rang.

"Hi, Simone. What a nice surprise," Lexi said, answering the call.

"Hi, Lexi. How are things going so far?" Simone inquired.

"Good. I'm eating some delicious French toast right now. You know, it's only 8 o'clock here, with the time change. How are things with you?"

Even though Lexi and Simone lived in the same house, she was still Lexi's landlord and they were never really close friends. It seemed a bit odd to Lexi that Simone was calling her, but then again, it was nice to be missed. Maybe Simone cared more about Lexi than she realized. Lexi hoped that was the case because since she'd been in Atlanta, she had a hard time making good friends.

"Everything here in Atlanta's normal. Are you sure nothing special's happening out there? I mean, other than French toast?" Simone was digging. What did she want?

"What are you asking me, Simone?"

"Oh, come on, Lexi. I saw you on the Internet with that gorgeous Sebastian Hawk. Holy shit! I couldn't believe my eyes. It was you, right?" Simone said excitedly.

"You saw me on the Internet? Where? What website?"

"So it *was* you! I knew it. Tell me all about him. What's he like. What happened? Oh my God. This is the most exciting thing EVER!!!"

"Calm down, Simone. He's just a person, you know. He was in the seat next to me. We got along really well, that's all," Lexi replied.

"Yeah, I can see how well you got along. There's

a picture of you straddling him while you're making out. And then there's a video of him feeling you up and you, well, doing the same to him while he's practically on top of you. The article with the picture said that the flight attendant was appalled by your behavior and threatened to have you two arrested for indecent exposure."

"WHAT? Patty! Oh my God! Simone, it's not true! There was this flight attendant, Patty something-or-other, who was flirting with Sebastian the whole time, but he wasn't paying much attention to her. You know how a jealous woman can be. She made it all up, well, not all of it. We did kiss," Lexi said in a slightly bragging way.

"So did you guys have sex?"

Lexi defended her behavior. "NO! I told you, we just kissed, well and maybe just a little more. But we were both REALLY DRUNK. You know they give you free liquor in first class, right?"

"But what about Greg?" Simone asked. "Did you guys break up?"

"No, of course not. Simone, this is not a big deal. So I kissed Sebastian Hawk? How often in life do you get a chance to be intimate with a celebrity? And Greg and I have only been going out a little while. It's not like we're engaged."

Lexi wanted to hear Simone's reaction so she could gauge how to speak to Greg, if he ever found out. It was unlikely that he would follow Hollywood gossip, but just in case it somehow got back to him.

"So you *were* intimate. I knew it!" Simone exclaimed.

"For the last time, NO! WE DID NOT HAVE SEX!" Lexi may have said that a little too loudly. Several of the people in the hotel's restaurant turned around and looked at her. Lexi was actually embarrassed. She got up from her table and walked down a hallway so she could speak with Simone in private.

"Simone, by intimate I simply meant that we kissed and got to know personal things about each other. We had some really honest moments and it was a nice experience sharing so much with someone I just met."

"Yeah, I saw how you shared."

It seemed as though Simone would not believe Lexi no matter what she told her.

"How many people do you think saw that Internet stuff?" Lexi asked.

"When I looked at it about ten minutes ago, it had close to 150,000 hits."

Oh my God! This is way out of hand, Lexi thought.

"Simone, please don't say anything to Greg. I'm hoping he won't find out and this can be our little secret, okay?"

"By *our* secret, you mean between you, me and the 149,999 other people who saw it?" Simone laughed.

"Yes, that's exactly what I mean. Okay? Can

you keep your trap shut? I don't want Greg to get hurt. I can't take back what I did, but I can try to pretend it never happened. Can you?" Lexi begged.

"Lexi, you're asking a lot of me. I never know anything juicy and now I know the biggest news of the day and you don't want me to talk?"

"It's not the biggest news of the day, Simone. Let's put it in perspective. I'm sure a country is at war somewhere and people are dying in tragic car accidents as we speak. Come on, now. It was just a little bit of kissing. Didn't you ever keep a harmless secret from Dale? How would you like it if I told him about those two hundred dollar designer shoes you just bought?"

"Lexi, are you blackmailing me?" Simone was stunned.

"Not at all. I'm just asking you to put the shoe on the other foot here, so to speak." Lexi tried to sound friendly so Simone would back off, but in actuality Lexi was getting very annoyed with Simone's persistence.

"Okay. I won't say anything to Greg, but–"

"Or to anyone who knows him or me, right?" Lexi interrupted.

"Yeah, right. Can I at least tell my mom? She doesn't really know you."

"Fine, tell your mom. But that's it! Go do something productive now. Did you get the carpets cleaned yet? I know Dale wanted you to do that while I was away."

"Yeah, yeah. Have a good rest of your trip.

I can't imagine it could get any better. I'm so jealous!"

"Bye, Simone."

"Bye, Lexi. Call me if something else happens!"

"I will, bye." When Lexi hung up, her stomach began to wrench. She headed back to her room to chug some Pepto Bismol and get ready to leave on the tour. But first, she knew what she had to do... call Greg.

Chapter 6 – Ramifications

"Hi Lexi. How's your day going so far?" Greg asked when he answered the phone.

"Hi. It's still early here. I'm about to meet up with my group in the lobby. Just thought I would call to let you know I'm still alive and thinking of you. How's your day?"

"That's very considerate of you. I tell everyone you're the sweetest girl I've ever known," Greg said kindly. "My day is okay. I'm getting ready for a business lunch with the Ramer Group. They own a real estate consortium and if we win their account, it could translate into a lot of business. I might have to work a little bit of extra time, just to give you a head's up."

"I know you have to work hard. I admire that about you. Don't ever worry about that. I'm not one of those clingy women."

"I know you're not, but I miss you when I'm

stuck in the office late at night and on weekends."

"Well, it's not a done deal yet, right? I mean, I hope you get it, but let's not worry about the ramifications, okay?"

"Yeah, you're right. Have fun today, sweetheart," Greg said warmly.

"You too, babe. Good luck. I know you're gonna knock 'em dead! Bye."

"Bye Lexi."

Lexi felt much worse after speaking with Greg. How could she betray his trust? He wasn't boring at all, and she felt guilty for accusing him of that. He was considerate, caring, mature and he genuinely adored her. What's bad about that? Nothing. That would be the end of Sebastian, she decided. Whether he called her or not, it was over, whatever *it* was.

When Sebastian arrived at his house, Matt was waiting outside his gate. They went into his Hollywood Hills home and settled into the kitchen area. Sebastian was starving and refused to utter a word to Matt until he had some sustenance. After eating an oatmeal chewy bar, a bowl of Rice Krispies cereal and a banana, Sebastian was ready to talk.

"Okay, so what do you want from me?" he asked Matt.

"I need details."

"I already told you what happened," Sebastian

explained.

"No, I mean what's her name? Are you going to see her again? Is she a girl from your past? Tell me everything!" Matt insisted.

"What, are you my priest?"

"No, I'm your publicist and if you want a little bit of heaven while still here on Earth, then you need my help, so spill."

"Fine. Her name's Lexi Lincoln. She's cute as can be, as you could probably tell by what you saw online. By the way, can I see it?"

"You haven't looked at it yet? What the hell am I going to do with you, Sebastian?"

"When was I supposed to look at it? I did what you said and left the hotel immediately. I had to wait in the smelly stairwell that led to the alley for, like, half an hour before Sam showed up. So give me a break, would ya?"

"Okay, sorry. Here it is." Matt pulled out his iPad and played it for Sebastian.

"Well?" Matt asked. "Now what do you think?"

"Damn, she's hot!"

"Sebastian, that's not the point here. Stay focused. What are we going to do about this?"

"I don't think I care. Leave it alone. I didn't do anything wrong. If you want to tell people the truth, then do that. Let them know that I was dumped by Amanda and I had every right to enjoy the company of another young lady."

"Who's gonna believe that?" Matt looked at Sebastian as though he was insane. "Are you drunk?"

"No, I'm not drunk, but my head still hurts so could you please just lighten up a little, man?" Sebastian insisted.

"Look, Sebastian, Amanda's people have already come out with a statement saying that she's devastated by your betrayal. So you see, even though she's the evil bitch in this situation, you're being painted as the cheating bastard. You can't afford to have your women fans hate you."

"What do you mean Amanda's people have issued a statement? How does she even know about this in St. Thomas? From what I could tell, the only news she was interested in there was whether or not she and Tom were climaxing."

"Be that as it may, her people got right on it and now we have to play catch-up," Matt explained.

"Okay, well, you're the expert here. What do you think we should do?" Sebastian asked.

"Let's start by you answering my questions about Lexi."

"Fine. She's a dental hygienist from Atlanta and she's here for a few days because she won a contest from a teeth whitening company. Okay? There's no need to make this into a bigger deal than it is. Now, how do we let the public know that I was really the one who had *my* heart stomped on?"

"That's it? You promise?" Matt pushed.

"YES, that's it. But she's a great girl and I'm

going to call her later to see if she wants to grab a bite tonight. Is that okay with you, Dad?"

"I don't appreciate the sarcasm, Sebastian. I'm just trying to do the job you pay me to do. And no, it's not okay with me if you see her again. Can't you just let things settle down with the Amanda situation before you start hooking up with other women? Could you do me that favor?" Matt insisted.

"Matt, do you understand what it's like to be in love with someone and then find out that the whole time they told you they loved you, they were actually running around behind your back with your friend? No, of course you don't, because this isn't a normal situation that happens to everyone. It's a shitty situation that just happened to me. I'm a victim, and you and the rest of the world need to treat me as such!" Sebastian became angry.

"Look, man. I hear what you're saying, and I do care, I really do, but it's not about whether or not you're hurting. It's about saving your fan base and subsequently saving your job. Do you hear what I'm saying? You may think it's a stupid part of the business, but it's the reality."

"Yeah, I know. It's just that Lexi understood me. She was sympathetic," Sebastian explained.

"Oh, is that it? I can be incredibly sympathetic. And so can my shrink. Do you want her number?"

"Go do your job, Matt, and leave me the hell alone, okay? I just want to go to bed and sleep."

"That's good. Stay in and get some rest. I'll

figure out how to spin this. You ARE the victim. When we get done with Amanda, she won't know what hit her!" Matt pronounced.

"No, I don't want you to annihilate her. Yeah, I'm pissed, but I did love her. Do you get that? I just want this to go away. Make it go away."

"Okay, one order of Houdini's disappearing act it is. Don't stress, Sebastian. I'll take care of everything."

Sebastian walked Matt to the door and then he went up to his bed and collapsed. How did this week turn into such a nightmare?

Lexi went down to the hotel lobby at 9:30 a.m., as she was told to do by the itinerary she found in her gift bag. There she met up with the other nineteen contest winners and the public relations people from Dental Dream Whitening. She couldn't believe that in the entire country she was among the top twenty sales people for their products. And that, of course, wasn't her main job. She felt quite proud.

After a brief check-in period, everyone was ushered onto a small tour bus. It was very luxurious and Lexi felt like a VIP riding in it. Their first stop was at Universal Studios where they were then given a private tour of the property. They were even brought onto some sound stages to see where television show tapings occurred. Lexi was having a great time until the tour guide started to talk about *Crime Days and Nights*. He went on and on about what a big hit the show was and how he was sorry that the show was on hiatus because they wouldn't be able to catch a glimpse of any of its stars. The women in the group all started to moan in disappointment. They wanted to meet that handsome Sebastian Hawk.

Lexi hated how she felt when Sebastian's name was brought up. It was only an hour or two earlier when she vowed to be true to Greg, yet she found herself longing for Sebastian. She knew realistically that she would probably never hear from him again. Celebrities – hell, men – were like that. But she enjoyed being with him and wanted more of him. Damn, temptation was a bitch!

Chapter 7 – Annihilation

When Sebastian woke up it was already four o'clock in the afternoon. His headache was down to a dull, annoying pain and for that he was grateful. He took a shower and then stared at his face in the mirror.

"Harvey, how did you let this happen?"

The head in the mirror didn't answer back, but it did shake in disapproval. *What's wrong with me?* he thought. *I'm twenty-eight years old. Shouldn't I be able to maintain a relationship with a nice woman by now? My player days have long been over. Hell, for the last six years, since I've been on this series, there've been no drugs and, aside from yesterday's overindulgence, no drunkenness. I think I'm a good guy and deserve a good life so what the hell am I doing wrong? Why was I sure Amanda was the one for me? Maybe I just wanted to be loved so badly, by anyone, that I've been settling.*

*Yeah, that must be it. It's like Lexi said, it's hard
to tell who's fake in this town. I shouldn't blame
myself. Love is hard, especially here.*

With that self-analysis session over, Sebastian
proceeded to get dressed and ready for the rest of
his day. The pep talk did him good. He decided he
wasn't going to dwell on his pain, but move forward
in a better direction. He picked up the phone and
made a very important call.

"Hello, thank you for calling the Marina Del Rey
Marriott, how may I direct your call?"

"Yes, hi, room 623 please?"

"The name of the guest, sir?"

"Lincoln. Lexi Lincoln," Sebastian said firmly.

"My pleasure. Have a nice evening."

The phone rang and rang, but Lexi didn't
answer. Finally, the voice messaging system
kicked in. Sebastian wasn't sure if he should leave
a message or not. In fact, he came very close to
hanging up, but then decided that he intended to
speak with her and she needed to know how to
reach him.

"Hi Lexi. It's Sebastian. I hope you had a good
time today. I was wondering if you're available to
get together later tonight, maybe for a bite in a real
restaurant? Call me back when you get this. My
number is 310-555-8966. Thanks."

Sebastian hadn't called a woman for a date in
many months, since he and Amanda got together,
and he was somewhat uncomfortable making
the call to Lexi. But he had feelings for her that

he simply couldn't deny. He found her warm smile and refreshing candor to be an irresistible combination. She was a *real* person. That's what he wanted. That's what he needed.

After hanging up, Sebastian checked his own messages. There were several from tabloid reporters. There was also a recent one from Matt asking Sebastian to call him, which he promptly did.

"Hey Matt. What's up?"

"Well, I'm glad you're not going to see Lexi again because this thing is really blowing up. I know, I know, I told you I could make it go away, but Amanda's people have sent stories to all of the television shows, Internet sites, papers and magazines. I don't know why she's on the offensive here, but she's going after your balls, man. Any idea why?" Matt asked.

"Well, see, that's the problem. I have no idea why that woman does any of the things she does. I guess she's just evil, and you can quote me on that," Sebastian growled.

"I have a theory. I think when she saw that you immediately found another girl, she got pissed. Women are like that. They always want to have their cake and eat it too, you know? I think she expected you to be rolled into a ball in your room crying your eyes out over her. And when that didn't happen, it made her furious. What do you think?"

Sebastian didn't want to tell Matt that he did curl into a ball and cry his eyes out. That's what he and Lexi were doing instead of having sex. But, of course, that would remain a secret.

"I have no answer, man. So what now?" Sebastian asked.

"I want permission to fight fire with fire. Will you let me do that? It might get ugly, but if I don't do something strong, your career could seriously suffer," Matt explained.

"What do you mean? Will Lexi get hurt by this?"

"Why do you care so much about a girl you met yesterday? Come on man, get a grip on reality. There are bigger issues at stake here than Lexi's feelings."

"No. I want to talk with her and see what she says before we go on a global attack. This does involve her and she's been the only decent person in my life in a long time, no offense, man."

"Alright. I'll call her and arrange a meeting for the three of us," Matt suggested.

"No way! You're not calling her. Besides, I already left her a message. When she calls me back, I'll discuss it with her."

"You called her? Come on Sebastian, you told me you wouldn't," Matt complained.

"Yeah, Matt, and you told me you could be Houdini and make all this disappear. I guess we're both liars," he replied.

"Call me the minute you get the go-ahead from her. Time is of the essence, okay?" Matt insisted.

"Fine, okay. I hope to speak with her soon. I'll

call you ASAP."

Sebastian wanted to keep himself busy, so he decided to go to the gym. Working out would be a good way to kill time while also burning off the anxiety he was feeling from all of the craziness in his life.

Lexi had a delightful day touring several of Hollywood's famous landmarks. She arrived back at her hotel at around 5:00 p.m., leaving her just enough time to freshen up for the swanky cocktail party reception that was being held for all of the contest winners in the hotel's lounge. Plans for the next day included dental seminars in the morning and then some free time for shopping and whatnot, until the big banquet at night, where she would receive her award. It was a fantastic itinerary and prize. Lexi was very happy.

Lexi changed into a short, red cocktail dress and was just about to go downstairs to the party when she noticed the flashing light on the phone in her room. She pushed the messages button and listened. Much to her shock it was Sebastian. What should she do? Should she call him, or should she ignore it and hold true to the promise she made to herself about Greg?

"Hi Sebastian. It's me, Lexi. I just got your message. Sorry I missed you. I had a lovely day, thanks for asking. I hope yours wasn't as bad as you expected. Anyway, I'm going to a cocktail party in the hotel's nightclub now. You're welcome to come if you want – at least I think you are. Actually, I'm not sure if it's a private function or not. Why don't you call me back when you can? My cell's 404-555-4012. Hope to talk to you soon. Bye!"

Lexi had a wonderful time at the party where she met more nice people from all over the country. She loved hearing about everyone's lives and how much they each enjoyed their jobs. She danced with all of them, the women and the men, in a big pit of happiness. What a blast! It was a few minutes before 9:00 p.m. when she left the party, feeling quite exhausted from the busy day. Lexi headed up to her room and found a surprise at her door.

"Hi Sebastian. What are you doing here?"

"Well, I was in the neighborhood." Sebastian smiled and stood up.

"How long have you been sitting there? Why didn't you call me or come into the party?" Lexi asked.

"I tried calling you, but you didn't answer. I left you a bunch of messages. The paparazzi followed me to the hotel and I didn't want to create a commotion at your event so I figured I'd just wait here for you to return. And here you are!" he said with a smile.

"Oh my gosh, this is such a surprise...a nice surprise," Lexi said while opening the door to her room. "You know, I think I saw some of those photographers in the lobby, but I didn't give them a second thought. It's Hollywood, after all."

"They do seem to be everywhere," he agreed.

Once they were in her room with the door closed they gave each other a hello hug. Then they sat on the chairs by the table where they had attempted to eat their dinner the previous night.

"So, tell me all about your day," Sebastian asked. Even though his words were genuine, Lexi could tell from the look on his face and his anxious behavior that he was the one who really wanted to do the talking. She returned the question to him.

"First tell me about yours."

"My day? Well, it's been strange, that's for sure," Sebastian said.

"What's wrong, Sebastian? I may not be a fake detective, but I'm a woman and all of my instincts are telling me that you're holding something back. Just spit it out, it'll be okay. I'm sure I can help you through it," she said in a reassuring manner.

"Lexi, you're amazing. I can't believe how giving you are. I feel really bad about what I'm about to ask, but here goes...Matt, my publicist, says that Amanda's people are doing everything they can to make me look like a terrible person. He thinks the best way to combat it is to release a ton of press countering Amanda's attacks."

"I'm not sure I understand. What's the big deal about that exactly?" Lexi asked with curiosity.

"It means that you and your name will forever be linked to me. The pictures and video of us making out will be everywhere – on TV, in magazines, you know, everywhere. People love shit like this."

"Me? I'm going to be everywhere? Oh no, I can't do that. What about Greg? That will be the end of us if he sees it!" Lexi said in an upset tone.

"I know. That's why I told Matt not to do anything until I spoke to you. The problem is that if I don't respond to Amanda's accusations, the whole world will think that I'm a cheating scumbag and my fans will abandon me. It could be the end of my career," Sebastian said with concern.

"Come on, you're being a bit dramatic here, don't you think? I mean, I get that you're an actor, so by definition you add drama to everything. But no one really loses their career for cheating on a girlfriend. I mean you guys weren't even married. Look at Brad Pitt. People still love him even though he dumped poor Jennifer Anniston."

"I DIDN'T CHEAT! But regardless of that fact, the truth is I'm not Brad Pitt, Lexi. I'm an actor on a TV show who's trying to keep his job. My business is all about ratings, and ratings come from fans. If my fans turn on me, I could be fired. The reality is that it may take a very long time before another great job comes along, if one this good ever does again."

"You could always become a dentist!" Lexi said jokingly.

Sebastian did not appreciate her sense of humor, not at that moment, which was clear from his serious expression.

"Sorry about that. Sometimes when I get nervous I make stupid jokes. I know this is a big deal for you, but it's a big deal for me too," Lexi explained.

"I know," he told her. "That's why I'm here talking to you about it. I really like you and I want us to be friends for a very long time. How can we stay friends and both get what we want – me a job and you a boyfriend?"

"Well, that's the magic question, isn't it. But we're smart people, I'm sure together we can come up with a solution," Lexi said optimistically.

"Do you have a computer here?" Sebastian asked.

"In my bag. Let me get it."

Lexi pulled out her laptop. While it was booting up she asked Sebastian to explain why he needed a computer.

"I just want to see how far the gossip has spread," he explained.

Lexi thought that made sense. They typed 'Sebastian Hawk' into the search engine and up came a long list of sites that contained their images. They clicked on one and the headline read, "Amanda Evans callously discarded by Sebastian Hawk and his new bird." Another site said, "Sebastian Hawk is really a swine."

"I think we have our answer," Lexi said sadly.

"What?"

"We're already all over the Internet. It would

be impossible for Greg not to get wind of this. You might as well at least try to save your career because my guy, I'm guessing, is already long gone."

Sebastian looked at Lexi and felt terrible. "Maybe not," he said. "It doesn't say your name and you can barely tell that it's you."

"Sure you can. My landlord called me this morning to say she saw me. Apparently, name or no name, people can make out that it's me making out!"

Lexi paused for a moment. She should have been more upset, but she had such a lovely day that her mood was still light enough to deal with things.

"Screw 'em!" she said while throwing her arms up in the air and walking away from the computer. "I don't care. Whatever happens, happens. That's just life, right? Go ahead and tell Matt to do whatever he wants. You have much more to lose than me, and I participated willingly. This is my own undoing. It's not your fault."

"Are you sure?" Sebastian wanted to make certain that she really meant it.

"Yes. How many times do I have to tell you? It's fine. I just hope you can come out okay after all of this. They say any publicity is good publicity, right? So maybe this will be a blessing in disguise. Most things are!"

"You have the best attitude of anyone I've ever met. Come here," Sebastian motioned to her. He grabbed Lexi and kissed her with every ounce of passion he could muster after such a draining day.

Since Greg was either already out of her life or would likely be gone soon, Lexi saw no reason to feel guilty about being with Sebastian – until she heard her phone beeping.

"Why don't you call Matt while I check my phone for messages? I can hear it beeping now. I guess it was too loud in the club," she said.

Sebastian called Matt and told him the good news, while Lexi listened to her six voicemail messages. Four were from Sebastian, just like he said. Another was from Simone wanting to know if anything else exciting had happened. And the last one, the dreaded one, was from Greg. Lexi reluctantly played the message.

"Hi, sweetheart. I hope you had a good day today. I wanted to tell you the great news. We got that new account! I wish you were here so we could celebrate! Call me when you can. Bye."

Shit! He didn't know, which meant Lexi just signed her own relationship's death warrant. She felt like an idiot. But what choice did she have? It wouldn't be right to let Sebastian's career plummet just because she was too ashamed to admit to what she'd done. She made her own bed and would have to lie in it. She decided she had to confess to Greg. That would be the only way to make things right, before he heard it from someone else – or worse yet, saw her on TV.

Chapter 8 – The Calls

Matt already had several press releases ready to go when Sebastian called and gave him permission to send them out. Matt pushed a button and instantly the world knew what Lexi Lincoln had been up to.

"This must be what the President feels like when he places orders to drop bombs on unsuspecting countries," Lexi said to Sebastian. "Guess what? It turns out that Greg doesn't know yet, and it's too late with the time difference for me to call him now. I'm going to hang on to the hope that I'll be the first to reach him in the morning."

"Lexi, I'm so sorry for you and Greg. I know how bad it feels to break up with someone you care about. I never meant for there to be any collateral damage, to use your analogy."

"I know you didn't. Plus, I started it all when I kissed you, remember? So don't stress. It's mostly my fault."

"You're right. I should be furious with you!" he said angrily.

Lexi couldn't tell if he was actually mad or not. He was an actor after. Was he really pissed at her?

"Are you? Are you mad at me?" Lexi hated when people didn't like her. She knew Greg would hate her, but if Sebastian hated her too, how much lower could she feel?

"Yes, I am. Now get over here and let me show you how much I hate you." Sebastian pulled his shirt off and then walked over to Lexi and unzipped her dress.

"Sebastian, really?" Lexi was surprised. He was toying with her emotions and the rollercoaster was rather exciting. "Oh my God!" she exclaimed as he slowly pulled her dress over her head, seductively running his hands along her sides.

Lexi stood there in her red bra and panties and black high heels. Sebastian was beyond ready for her. In one swift motion he lifted her off the floor and gingerly placed her on top of the puffy bed. Lexi looked shocked, but happy. Sebastian removed his shoes, pants, and socks and Lexi helped him out of his underwear. Then he took off her shoes and began kissing her body, starting with her toes. He made it up to the middle of her thigh when his phone rang.

"Ignore it," he told Lexi. And she did.

Until it rang again. And then again. By then Sebastian had Lexi's panties in his teeth, having just slipped them down her legs.

"Maybe you should get it. It might be important," Lexi said reluctantly.

"I don't care."

Lexi's body was writhing in anticipation as Sebastian removed her bra.

Then the hotel room's phone rang.

"Holy shit!" Sebastian said.

"What do you think?" Lexi asked. She figured that the mood was rapidly becoming ruined anyway so he might as well take the call. He thought the same thing.

Sebastian stood up and went over to the hotel phone. "What, Matt? WHAT?" he barked into the phone.

"Stay away from Mary," the voice said, and then the caller hung up.

"That was weird," Sebastian said.

"Did Matt get cut off?" she asked.

"Wait a minute. Let me check my cell phone," he told her.

Sebastian walked across the room naked. His body was perfect in Lexi's eyes and she was ready to have him inside her. She was impatient and thought why did that have to be happening NOW?!

"Oh no!" Sebastian exclaimed.

Lexi sat up. "What did Matt want?" she asked. "What could be so important that he had to keep calling you?"

"It wasn't Matt. You'd better listen to this."

Sebastian brought his phone over to the bed

and then turned the speakerphone on while he played back his voicemail. "Stay away from Mary. She's mine."

All three messages were the same.

Lexi began to cry and shiver immediately. "The Leech!" she screamed. Sebastian wrapped Lexi in a blanket and held her tight, trying to get her to stop shaking. Unlike when she was being questioned by the TSA at the airport, no amount of happy thoughts could reduce the stress she was feeling at that moment.

"Was that him on the hotel phone, too?" she asked, her voice quivering.

"Yeah, I think so."

"Then he knows where we are. We'd better get out of here...now!" Lexi insisted.

Lexi and Sebastian got dressed frantically.

"Hold on a second, Lexi. Why don't we just call the police?" Sebastian suggested rationally.

"They're no help, believe me," she told him. "I've got to get out of here."

"I'll protect you, Lexi." Even though Sebastian said it, he didn't really believe he could do it. What did he know about dealing with deranged lunatics? He could barely manage his ex-girlfriend.

"I'll call Sam and as soon as he says he's here, we can take the side stairwell and meet in the alley," Sebastian said.

"Okay. Wait. No. I think we should go out the front because there will be more people around. If The Leech is here, he won't do anything in front of everyone, right?" Lexi said.

"Yeah, that makes sense. I'm calling Sam."

After he hung up with Sam, Sebastian called his manager, Wayne Iverson.

"Wayne, it's Sebastian."

"Hi Sebastian. Sorry about everything you're going through with Amanda, but I know with Matt on top of things, it'll all work out."

"Yeah, thanks. That's not actually why I'm calling," Sebastian said. His tone was intense.

"Okay. What then?" Wayne asked.

"I need a bodyguard, immediately," Sebastian told him.

"Why? What happened?"

"I can't go into details now, but can you have someone meet me at my house ASAP?" Sebastian asked.

"Are you all right?" Wayne was concerned. Sebastian was usually a calm guy so the fact that he sounded unnerved was unsettling to Wayne.

"So far."

"Okay. I'll make a couple of calls and get someone there as soon as I can. Be careful in the meantime," Wayne told him.

"Thanks."

Sebastian went back to Lexi's computer to see what was happening with the story since Matt's press releases came out. He clicked on one link and the headline said, "Mr. Hawk and Ms. Lincoln fly the friendly skies." That was no different than the bad reports from earlier, Sebastian thought, except it included Lexi's name. Shit!

He clicked another link, "Evans digs her claws into Hawk." That's better. Nice one Matt!

On the next website he visited, there were two photos. One was a picture of Sebastian walking into the Marriott and then a line was drawn and there was a shot of Lexi in the hotel's lobby. The headline said, "Marina Del Rey hook-up for Hawk."

"That must be how The Leech found me," Lexi surmised. "Look, it clearly says Marriott in the photo. Oh my God. I can't believe after two years he's still after me."

"It's crazy!" Sebastian agreed.

"He's crazy. I told you."

They were both scared when the phone rang. But it was Sam calling to let Sebastian know that he was downstairs with the car. Sebastian and Lexi strategized about what to do next. Should they go down together? That would just feed the photogs. However, if they went separately, that could be dangerous for Lexi. They decided to have Sam come up to their room and walk back down with them. Safety in numbers, they figured.

Even though they were expecting him, Lexi and Sebastian both jumped a bit when Sam knocked on the hotel room's door. After looking through the peephole, Sebastian opened it and then they all walked quickly to the elevator. Thankfully, it was still on the 6th floor since Sam had just gotten out of it. When they reached the lobby only one paparazzi was left. He snapped a bunch of pictures, but Sam was in all of them so they were hopefully unusable.

The drive to Sebastian's house seemed longer than usual for Sebastian. He was holding Lexi's hand, but couldn't help thinking about how she was slowly ruining his life. He felt bad for thinking that, and it wasn't entirely true since it was Amanda who started the whole chain of events. But if Lexi hadn't been seated next to him on the airplane, they both would have been better off.

Lexi was very freaked out. Even though this was not her first encounter with The Leech, it had been such a long time since her ordeal with him that she had forgotten the terror his voice brought her.

"We're here," Sebastian whispered to Lexi. "See, I have an iron gate in my driveway. You'll be safe."

When they went inside Lexi finally exhaled. She did feel safer, but she was still leery of The Leech.

A buzzer sounded.

"It's okay, Lexi. That's just the gate. It's probably the bodyguard," Sebastian reassured her.

"Hello?" Sebastian spoke into the intercom.

"Hello, sir. This is Marcus Smith from Stealth Security. Mr. Iverson sent me."

Sebastian pushed a button that opened the gate and then he went to the door to let Marcus in. Marcus was a large man with a large weapon strapped to his side. Lexi had never been that close to such a big gun, and she lived in Georgia. She definitely felt safer with him there.

Marcus assured them that he would secure the perimeter so they could get a good night's rest. In the morning his boss would come to speak with them about their concerns.

Lexi and Sebastian went up to Sebastian's room. They changed for bed. She put on her pink lace nightshirt and he wore a pair of dark blue boxers.

"Are you going to be okay?" Sebastian asked as they lay in bed facing each other.

"Yes. Thank you so much. Are you going to be okay?" she asked him.

"Who the hell knows, right? After the last few days I've had, I seriously don't think things could get any worse."

"I'm so sorry, Sebastian," Lexi said sincerely.

"It's okay. Try to get some sleep."

She kissed him. "Goodnight, my knight in shining armor."

"Well, I guess that's better than your fake detective!" he chuckled.

She smiled and they eventually fell asleep.

Chapter 9 – Room 623

Lexi and Sebastian had just finished eating breakfast when Bruno Caparelli, the owner of Stealth Security, and Victor, a daytime guard, arrived at 10:00 a.m. on the dot. They all sat in the living room, each in a different club chair, and talked about their options.

"It sounds like this guy is all bark and no bite," Bruno announced. "I wouldn't worry too much about him. All he's done is make some phone calls and post some Internet messages, right? He could've done that from anywhere in the world. It doesn't mean he's here in Los Angeles. I don't think he's much of a physical threat to either of you. However, until a little more time has passed and he's either backed off or escalated things, I think it's wise to keep one of our bodyguards with you at all times," he advised.

They thanked Bruno for his assistance

and said goodbye to him and Marcus. Lexi and Sebastian had spent most of the morning on the Internet. The Leech had been busy. He made posts to many of the sites they were on, writing over and over again those same creepy words he spoke into the phone, "Stay away from Mary. She's mine."

It was close to 11:00 a.m. and Lexi, who had missed many of the teeth whitening workshops, was starting to relax.

"Do you think it'll be okay if I go back to the hotel to meet up with my group? I might be able to make it there in time for one of the talks," she said to Sebastian.

"I think at this point, with the traffic and all, you might as well take the entire morning off. It's not worth going all the way over there just for an hour, don't you agree?"

"Yeah, I guess you're right. So what were you going to do today?" Lexi asked Sebastian.

"What I had planned for today was lying on the beach in St. Thomas next to the woman I loved. But we all know that isn't going to happen," he said in a complaining tone. "It looks like I have some free time, too."

"The woman you loved? I guess I didn't realize that you and Amanda were in love. Oh, Sebastian. I feel so bad for you."

"*We* weren't in love, evidently," he corrected her. "Only I was."

Lexi looked at Sebastian and he got up and walked into the other room. She decided to give him some space. She had already imposed so much, she thought the least she could do was allow him to have privacy in his own home.

Lexi walked around Sebastian's living room and admired the many nice photos he had on the tables and walls. One that caught her interest showed Sebastian holding an award while standing between an older couple, who she figured were his parents. *They must be so proud of him*, she thought. *And they look like such nice people.*

As she walked to the other side of the room, she saw the actual award. *Oh my God! It's an Emmy!* For some reason it never occurred to Lexi that Sebastian was so talented. Suddenly she felt bad for teasing him so much about being an actor. Apparently, he was a great actor. *Wow! How impressive!*

Finally, Lexi's mind made its way back to reality and it dawned on her that she never called Greg.

"Oh no!" she said aloud in an empty room. "Greg!"

Lexi went searching for her purse because that's where she kept her phone. Where was it? She looked high and low and had Victor looking too.

Sebastian saw them hunting around his house. "What are you doing?"

"I can't find my purse," Lexi explained.

"Did you look in your suitcase?" he asked.

"Of course I did. That's the first place I looked,"

she snapped. They sounded like a couple.

"When was the last time you remember seeing it?" he asked her.

"I don't know. Everything's been such a blur," she huffed.

"Okay, calm down. I'm sure it's here somewhere. We'll find it. Let me think for a minute."

Lexi and Victor continued to search while Sebastian used his talent for recalling details to retrace their steps.

"I don't think you had it when we were in Sam's car. And I haven't seen it here in my house. I bet it's still at the hotel," he declared.

"Really? You think it's at the hotel?" She was surprised.

"Yeah, I do."

"Then we have to go there to get it. I mean, I have to go get it. You don't have to come. I've already caused you enough trouble," she said. "Why don't you relax and watch some TV or something? I shouldn't be long."

"You know, that sounds like a good idea. I'll have Victor go with you to make sure you're okay. I've actually got some work that I might as well take care of. Is that alright?" he asked.

"Of course."

"Here, Vic." Sebastian threw a set of car keys to Victor. "You can drive her, right?"

"Yes sir," Victor replied.

"Thanks, Victor. It shouldn't take very long.

Once I'm there I'll just pop into the room, grab my purse and then we can go," Lexi told him.

"No problem ma'am."

Damn, there was that stupid ma'am word again.

"Victor, please call me Lexi," she said.

"Okay, Lexi."

They left for the hotel and Sebastian did as Lexi suggested. He relaxed, read the paper and watched TV. He intentionally avoided any articles or programs that might be talking about him, which led him to watch Sherlock Holmes on cable. He justified it as research for his character.

Lexi and Victor entered the hotel together. As she walked across the lobby she heard someone call her name. It was a man's voice. She recognized it immediately and got very nervous.

"Greg? What are you doing here?" she asked. She was shocked to see him.

"Hi, sweetheart." He looked at Victor and then gave his girlfriend a kiss and a hug. "Who's he?"

"Greg, it's such a surprise to see you! This is my friend, Victor," Lexi said trying to sound casual.

Greg shook Victor's large hand. "Are you a contest winner, too?" he asked him.

Before Victor could respond, Lexi interrupted.

"Greg, I still can't believe you're here!"

"It felt so good to win that account yesterday that I just imagined how it must feel for you to win your award. I wanted to be with you tonight when you receive it. I realized that these wonderful moments are best when shared with people you care about," he said sweetly.

"Aw, you're the best!" Lexi hugged Greg very firmly. "When did you get here?"

"I just arrived. You have perfect timing," he said smiling.

"Let's go up to my room," Lexi said. "Victor, I'll see you later in the lobby, okay?" She looked at Victor with an expression to indicate that she would be fine. Of course Victor had no idea who Greg was, but he did as he was asked and waited for Lexi in the lobby. He knew Bruno would be mad if he found out that he did not accompany the client, but she specifically told him to stay put so he figured he was clear of any guilt should something happen to Lexi.

Greg and Lexi made small talk in the elevator and then went into room 623. Lexi immediately saw her purse under the desk chair, but before she retrieved it, she took a few moments to kiss Greg properly. She knew she had to have a talk with him and it made her very sad to think about how her news would upset him. He's such a great guy.

"What are you doing today?" Greg genuinely wanted to know. "Can I join you for anything?"

"Babe, I need to talk with you about something.

"Okay," Greg said.

Lexi and Greg sat on the edge of the bed. She held his hand and then looked into his eyes. Greg had no idea what was about to come out of her mouth.

"Well, you see, there's a whole bunch of stuff going on that isn't good and I have to tell you," Lexi rambled.

"What?"

"Sorry. Let me take a moment to gather my thoughts." Lexi took a couple of deep breaths.

"Have you ever heard of the show *Crime Days and Nights*?" Lexi asked him.

"Yeah. I love it, why? Did you get to see them filming it? What a thrill that would be," Greg said excitedly.

"No, they're on hiatus now. But I did meet one of the actors from the show. His name's Sebastian Hawk. I'm not sure which character he plays."

"You met James? Lexi, he's the best! That guy can solve any crime no matter how few clues there are. On one episode, James discovered that the murderer was a trained dog!"

"Okay, so you know who he is, good. See, here's the thing. On my flight over here I was in the seat next to him."

Greg interrupted. "YOU SAT NEXT TO JAMES GILBERT? I would have killed for that seat!" Greg said with envy.

"His name's Sebastian, Greg. Anyway, please let me finish."

"Okay."

"Sebastian is a really nice guy and I guess he's a good actor too. Well, on our flight he was on his way back from surprising his girlfriend in St. Thomas, except when he got there he found her with another man. He was devastated so we shared some drinks together to help him deal with it."

"You mean, he–"

"Greg! Let me finish, please!" Lexi interrupted Greg. She felt bad for doing it, but if she didn't get this off her chest now, it would never happen.

"Okay," Greg complied.

"We both got very drunk – you know they give you free drinks in first class, right? Anyway, we kind of kissed a little, but it meant nothing, really. You're the guy for me," Lexi insisted.

"Slow down. You kissed James, I mean Sebastian? I know I should be angry with you, but I'm kind of strangely proud. He's a huge heartthrob and he kissed my girlfriend...Cool!"

"Cool? Are you kidding?" Lexi couldn't believe her ears. "Aren't you even a little jealous? Don't you care if I kiss other men? Have you been kissing other women?"

"Of course I care if you kiss other men, and *no*, I don't kiss other women. You're my number one girl. But how could I be jealous of James Gilbert? He's way out of my league and he's way out of yours. There's nothing to be jealous about. He was drunk and took advantage of an opportunity. That's what men do. He could never really be interested in someone like you," Greg said honestly.

"Someone like ME? Are you fucking kidding

me? What do you mean by that?" Lexi shouted. She stood up, outraged.

"Calm down, Lexi. There's no need to use that kind of language. I didn't mean anything bad by that. I just meant that guys like him are used to going out with gorgeous actresses and, even though *I* think you're beautiful, you're not glamorous like they are. That's all I'm saying."

"That's all you're saying? I can't believe that's how you think of me, your 'number one girl.' You know what Greg, you might be a wonderful guy, but you're also an asshole! I think you should go back to Atlanta and call your number two girl because she's just been promoted to number one!"

"Come on, Lexi. You don't mean that. I don't know what I'm saying. I think you're pretty and sweet and perfect." Greg walked over to Lexi to hug her but she pulled away. "I'm a guy. I say dumb stuff sometimes. I'm sorry."

Lexi shook her head. "Men. You're all so dumb, that's true."

"Come on. Tonight's your big night and it's going to be wonderful, you'll see. We'll have a fabulous time together. I promise to make it up to you," Greg said.

"There's more I have to tell you." Lexi continued.

"Did you have sex with him, Lexi? That's NOT cool!"

Lexi was happy that technically she could respond honestly to that question, "No, we never had sex."

"Okay, so what else do you need to tell me?"

"Where do I begin?" Lexi sighed. "There are pictures and a video of us from the flight that a jealous flight attendant posted on the Internet. And because Sebastian just broke up with his girlfriend, the media is having a frenzy with it."

"Oh, Lexi. This must be so embarrassing for you," Greg told her.

Somehow Lexi got the impression that Greg thought she was ashamed for being *played* by a celebrity. She was sure that Greg was going to tell all his guy friends to watch the video of his girlfriend and James.

"So you don't care?" she asked.

"I told you, if it had been with anyone else, I would be furious. But I understand."

Lexi realized that she should stop pressing the matter. The fact that Greg was okay with her making out with another man was troubling, for sure, but it was by far the best response she could have hoped for. She picked up her purse and walked to the door.

"Do you want to meet him?" she asked.

"For real? You know where he lives?"

"Yes, we're friends now. Victor works for him. I'll tell you all about it on the ride over to his house. There's still something else you need to know."

Chapter 10 – Meeting "James"

Lexi explained about The Leech to Greg during their car ride to Sebastian's house. Greg expressed concern for Lexi, but truthfully, he seemed to be a bit more focused on meeting the famous Sebastian Hawk, a.k.a. James Gilbert.

It felt strange for Lexi to just walk into Sebastian's house, so she rang the bell, with Greg and Victor standing beside her. Sebastian opened the door and looked at the trio. *Who the hell is that guy*, he wondered.

"Hi, Sebastian. I found my purse. You were right," Lexi said as she walked into his house. Greg and Victor trailed behind her. Victor immediately left them to check for locked windows and doors.

"Um, Sebastian, this is Greg, from Atlanta. He surprised me and came to join me for tonight's awards' banquet," Lexi said in a manner she hoped wouldn't let on to Greg that she and Sebastian were anything more than friends.

Sebastian put out his hand and Greg grabbed hold of it and gave him a firm handshake. Greg was so excited that words came flying out of his mouth.

"It's so great to meet you James, I mean Sebastian. I'm a HUGE fan of yours. I think James is the best character on TV and you are the most impressive detective I've ever seen." His enthusiasm was that of a teenage girl meeting Justin Bieber. Greg was ridiculously star struck.

"Hi, man. Nice to meet you," Sebastian said with a bewildered look on his face. "Lexi, can I speak with you in the kitchen? Greg, why don't you make yourself at home in the living room. It's over there on the right."

Greg walked happily and wide-eyed off to the living room.

Lexi started rambling the minute they got to the kitchen. "I know, I know, Sebastian. I'm so sorry. He was in the lobby when I got to the hotel and I didn't know what else to do. I told him about us kissing and he didn't seem to care. He was more concerned with meeting you, can you believe that? It kind of hurt my feelings."

"Well –"

"And I couldn't stay at the hotel because of The Leech. Maybe I should just get on a flight with Greg and go home to Atlanta to get out of your hair, but I really want to get my award. Is that dumb? I'm so, so sorry for messing up your life. I'm just totally confused."

"Lexi. Take a breath," Sebastian said, trying to take in all that she was telling him.

"Yeah, okay, sorry. I guess I'm kind of stressed."

"Of course you're stressed. But what am I supposed to do with this guy? I don't mind having you here – actually, you know I like your company – but this is way beyond weird, even for LA!"

"You're right. What do you think I should do?" Lexi asked.

"What do you want to do?"

Sebastian was hoping the answer would be that Lexi would send Greg packing, but he didn't hold out much hope for that since the guy flew across the country to be with her.

"Wow, I never even considered what I want. I don't know, let me think for a minute." After a brief pause, she looked into Sebastian's bright blue eyes and asked him a very important question. "Did you really mean it when you said you like my company? Do you really like me or are you just helping me because of my situation?"

Sebastian looked back into Lexi's big brown eyes and considered her question. Did he like her or was he simply being a good guy and trying to help her? Was he feeling things for Lexi because he was on the rebound or did he have actual feelings for this adorable, awkward, ballsy woman?

"Oh!" Lexi said when Sebastian released her from his kiss.

"I really like having you around," he told her, in case kissing her didn't make that clear.

"So what do I do with Greg? This is so uncomfortable," Lexi admitted.

"Why don't you take him to your banquet, get your award and then Sam can drive him to the airport. Tell him that you have to finish up some stuff with me because of the PR mess that's going on. Then, you come back here for the night and we can see where things go."

"I don't know. Does that make me a terrible person, lying to him like that?"

"How is that lying? You and I do need to figure things out. Plus, you still have that weird leech guy after you – and he might be after me. We have things to take care of, Lexi."

"Yeah, you're right. Do you think there'll be a flight available tonight for Greg?"

"There's usually a red-eye that goes to the east coast. Go and talk to him."

"I'm scared. I've got an idea, why don't *you* talk to him, Sebastian? Anything you tell him will sound wonderful coming from you. He likes me, but I seriously think he's in love with you!"

Lexi smiled at Sebastian. Her smile did it again. Sebastian went into the living room to talk with Greg.

While the men were in the living room, Lexi opened her purse and pulled out her phone. It was beeping. 72 voice messages and 51 texts. Crap! She didn't even know her phone could hold that much stuff. She sat down on a kitchen stool and began to read the texts. The first was a real surprise.

"Lexi, it's Mom. I saw you on TV. You're famous! Call me when you can. I'm so proud of you."

She's proud of me? What an odd thing to say to your daughter who got caught drunk and making out with a stranger in a public place. Man, my family is messed up, Lexi thought.

Then there were three texts from Simone that Lexi didn't bother to read. Another text from her boss who was wondering how LA was treating her. One from her co-worker who saw her on the Internet. And a whole bunch, more than she could count, from The Leech. Yup, he found her number. Lexi knew it was only a matter of time. After all, he had found Sebastian's number and it's really hard to get a hold of celebrities' private information.

Lexi was surprised that seeing the words *"Mary, I'm coming for you. You're mine,"* over and over again didn't send her into a tizzy. At that moment she somehow took it in stride. She felt very safe at Sebastian's. There were three men in the house with her and one had a huge gun.

The voice messages were about the same as the texts, except hearing The Leech's voice finally hit a nerve and she became quite upset. When Sebastian returned to the kitchen he found Lexi bent over the counter crying.

"I told him. It's okay," Sebastian said to Lexi. "He'll go with you to the thing tonight and then fly right home. You don't have to cry," Sebastian said tenderly.

"No, that's not it. There are over a hundred messages on my phone from The Leech. He's found me!" she said while crying.

Sebastian hugged Lexi and tried to comfort her any way he could. He reminded her about what Bruno had said. "He could be anywhere in the world. Just because he's calling doesn't mean he's here and is going to hurt you," Sebastian tried to reassure her.

The truth, however, was that Sebastian was pretty freaked out by the news. The Leech had certainly earned his nickname. He was not letting up.

"Come into the living room. Let's talk with Victor and Greg about this. Together the four of us can probably come up with a good plan."

Lexi was impressed at how level-headed Sebastian was in times of crisis. She admired his ability to stop and think things through before reacting, just as he had when the Internet thing happened. Maybe being a fake detective had taught him a few things.

Sebastian went to find Victor while Lexi walked into the living room where Greg was sitting patiently. Greg looked at Lexi, saw her bloodshot eyes, and immediately ran to her.

"What is it, sweetheart?" he asked.

"The Leech. He got my phone number. He left me like, a hundred texts and voice messages saying that 'he's coming and I'm his,' whatever that means."

Greg finally began to get that this was a dangerous situation for Lexi. "That's scary! I'm sorry, sweetie. I didn't realize that this guy was so crazy. Thank goodness Victor is here for us, I mean you."

"I told you The Leech was horrible when we were in the car, but all you cared about was meeting your precious James!" she said angrily between sobs.

"You're right, you did. I suppose I thought you were exaggerating. I should have known better than that. You never lie," Greg said.

Lexi let that comment slide. She no longer had any guilt about lying to Greg about her feelings for Sebastian because she thought his behavior all day was so bizarre. She was beginning to think that he was a major wimp. *Did she really want a man like that? Even if he was a nice man who made a good living?*

When Sebastian and Victor walked into the room they found Lexi sitting on the sofa next to Greg. Greg had his arm around her. It pissed Sebastian off, and that bout of jealousy really surprised him. He'd only known this girl for a few days, so why was he reacting so intensely?

Victor ran the meeting. "Okay, here's what we're going to do," he said in his deep voice. "Tonight, when Marcus comes, he will accompany all of you to Lexi's banquet in the hotel."

"Wait, why am I going?" Sebastian asked.

"It will be easier to protect all of you if you stay together," Victor explained. "Then, Sam will drive Greg to the airport, and Lexi and Sebastian will return here with Marcus. Okay?"

"No, it's not okay," Greg said firmly.

He surprised everyone with his noncompliance.

"Lexi is my girlfriend and I need to be here to help look after her. If this leech guy is really a threat to her, then I want to take him on myself."

Wow! Lexi was floored by Greg's words. He was so macho. So brave. So out of character.

Sebastian was less impressed. He was annoyed. Not only was he expected to go to a stupid banquet, but then he would have to sleep alone while this Greg dork was with Lexi in his guest room. No way!

"Um, excuse me, but do I get a say in this?" Sebastian piped in. He finally had about as much as he could take.

"What do you think, Sebastian?" Lexi asked gently.

"I think this is all ridiculous! Greg, go to the banquet and then go home! Lexi will be fine. I'm spending a lot of money to have professionals protect her. Also, I'm not going to the hotel for the banquet. I'll be perfectly safe here. That's what I think!"

Lexi was also surprised by Sebastian's reaction. He was so adamant.

It was Lexi's turn to say what she thought,

but she was interrupted by the ringing of the home phone. Sebastian let it go to the machine, but he jumped up when he heard the start of the message: "Hi Honey. I'm back. We need to talk. If you're there, pick up!"

Chapter 11 – Ideas

Sebastian was in the other room for nearly half an hour talking on the phone with Amanda. She was eager to discuss their publicity situation, but all Sebastian wanted from her was a sincere apology. However, Amanda didn't offer any words of consolation. Instead, she was very self-focused. Even when Sebastian told her about all of the crazy things going on in his life with The Leech, she didn't seem to care. When he hung up the phone, he felt even more hurt and disappointed than before. He put his feelings to the back of his mind and returned to the living room ready to deal with the business at hand.

"Okay," Sebastian started right back in, "I've been thinking about this whole leech thing and I think we're taking the wrong approach."

"What do you mean?" Victor asked.

"We've been on the defensive. I think we should

go on the offensive."

"Yes! That's what James would do," Greg agreed.

"Right. What I really want to do is find The Leech and put an end to all of this. Right now, he has the power. It's time it shifts to us!"

Sebastian's idea was so smart it made Lexi swoon. She felt her heart beat a little faster. *This man is one in a million*, she thought.

"How do we do that?" Lexi asked.

"We find him. He's been all over the computer. I used to study computers a few years back and it's still kind of a hobby of mine. If I can find his IP address, we can locate him. Also, I realized that since we know his name, why don't we do a search for him on the Internet. That's an even easier way to find him."

"It sounds so simple," Lexi said. "Oh my God, Sebastian, you're a genius. I wish I would've known you two years ago when all of this started. We could have whooped his ass back then and put an end to his harassment for good."

"Thanks, Lexi. But it just takes a moment away from a situation to see things clearly. When I was on the phone – you all must have figured out by now that the call was Amanda – she was giving me some bullshit story so my mind was wandering. As I was telling her about The Leech it occurred to me how to solve this problem," he explained.

"Oh, so you think you two won't be getting back together?" Lexi inquired. She really wanted to know even though she felt like it was none of her business. Still, that didn't stop her from asking.

"It doesn't look good, but I never say never. Someone taught me that if you get hurt once, that's not a good enough reason to quit something, or someone, forever," Sebastian said, looking at Lexi.

She was an idiot. Why did she ever tell him that?

"Sir, what do you want us to do?" Victor asked. He was a big, burly guy who was very good at playing defense. Sebastian wasn't so sure that offense would be Victor's strength.

"Victor, you keep doing what you're doing. Check the house. Keep us safe."

"Yes, sir," he said as he got up to inspect the home's security yet again.

"What about me?" Greg asked.

"Greg, you're an accountant right?"

"Yes I am," he said proudly.

Sebastian thought about what skills set Greg brought to the table and how he could be useful in their situation. He came up with nothing. The only thing Greg had going for him was his male voice.

"Here's what I think you should do. Call Travis Orrington's family and say that you're an old high school friend of his trying to get in touch with him. See if they'll tell you where he is. Lexi can give you his specifics so it seems real, right Lexi? You must know something about his family and where this guy went to school."

"It's been a couple of years and we only went on three dates, but I'll try my best to recall that information. What a great idea," she said.

"I'm going to the computer in my office. Come in when you guys have some news. Why don't you use your cell phone, Greg, since that's the one number The Leech doesn't seem to have? There's a pen and notepad on the table in the kitchen."

Sebastian was very direct and managerial. Greg was excited to be working for him. Lexi was just happy to try to stop The Leech before things got worse.

Lexi and Greg went into the kitchen and talked. She told Greg where she met Travis, back in Arizona where she used to live. As she reflected upon their dates, Lexi remembered that Travis attended St. Nicholas High School. That stuck in her mind because it made her think of Santa Claus and presents. Some gift he was!

Greg called directory assistance for information and found the city in Arizona where the high school was located. Armed with that information, he then called 411 again to ask for any listings they had for Orrington, Travis or otherwise.

"Hello ma'am. Sorry to interrupt your afternoon. But I was wondering if you're related to my old buddy, Travis Orrington?" Greg was very smooth.

"He's my son, who is this? Why do you want to know about Travis?" she asked suspiciously.

"Like I said, we were friends back at St.

Nicholas' and I've lost touch with him. I'd love to call Travis so we could catch up and talk about old times."

"Oh, isn't that nice? I think that would be very good for him," she said. "But I'm not sure if he's allowed to have calls."

"What do you mean?" Greg asked. He thought maybe the guy worked for some secret governmental agency, which would make it really hard to reach him.

"He's at Rolling Pines in Fontana, California."

"Rolling Pines? Thanks. Is that the name of his condo?" Greg asked.

"Oh dear. You don't know?" Mrs. Orrington said.

"Know what?"

"Travis has been under psychiatric care for the last year and a half. I think it would be such a wonderful thing for an old friend like you to go and visit him, if you could. Maybe it would help with his recovery," she said with hope in her voice.

"Yes, ma'am. I'll try to get in touch with him there. Maybe it will help. Thank you. Goodbye," Greg told her.

"Goodbye."

Greg shared the information with Lexi.

"Sebastian's a genius! And you were magnificent!" Lexi said with glee as she wrapped her arms around Greg. "Let's go tell Sebastian the good news."

Lexi bounced into Sebastian's office full of

excitement. "He's locked away in a loony bin!" she announced.

Sebastian looked up from his computer. "I found Travis' posts all over the Internet, but your news puts an end to everything, doesn't it? It looks like Bruno was right! This guy's just a nuisance, but no threat whatsoever."

"Woohoo!" Lexi exclaimed. She began to spin with her arms outstretched, just like a little girl does when twirling in the park. Her face was filled with joy and her dimple was clearly visible. *My God she's adorable*, Sebastian thought.

"Victor!" Sebastian hollered. In a split second Victor showed up at the door to Sebastian's office with his gun drawn. Lexi jumped back. They all learned that it's not wise to scream for your bodyguard unless you're really in trouble.

"Put your gun away. It's okay, Victor. It's over," Sebastian said calmly.

"Yeah, I found him," Greg announced proudly. He felt like a hero, but Lexi knew it was really Sebastian's idea that made everything possible.

"You can go home, now," Sebastian told Victor. "Tell Bruno to send the bill to Wayne, my manager."

"Yes, sir." Victor vacated the premises in no time flat.

"How about some champagne to celebrate?" Sebastian suggested.

"I'm buying," Greg insisted. He was showing off for his idol.

"Where should we go?" Lexi asked. "It's only 4:30 in the afternoon."

"I know a nice place nearby. Why doesn't everyone take a moment to freshen up and I'll meet you by the front door in fifteen minutes?" Sebastian suggested.

"Sounds wonderful," Lexi said smiling.

She went up to Sebastian's bedroom to get her things. Greg followed her there.

"Why is your bag in *his* room?" Greg asked.

"Oh, I stayed here last night. I thought I told you that earlier. The Leech was after me and I was too afraid to be alone. Plus, Sebastian hired a bodyguard. So this felt very safe," she explained as she went through the clothes in her bag.

Greg picked up Lexi's nightshirt which was strewn across the bed and tangled in some of the covers.

"What's this doing here? Lexi, what aren't you telling me?" Greg's voice began to get louder and she could see that he was heating up.

"It's nothing. I stayed up here to feel safe, that's all," she said calmly.

"Did he stay here with you?"

"Yeah."

"You slept with him? Lexi, you LIED to me?"

"Yes, I mean NO! I stayed in the same bed with him, but we never had sex, I told you that," she insisted. But Lexi couldn't look Greg directly in the eyes when she spoke because she knew it was a half-truth. Greg noticed her body language.

He stormed out of the bedroom and went from room to room looking for Sebastian. When he found him in his office, Greg walked right over to Sebastian who was sitting behind his large black desk and, without saying a word, smacked Sebastian across the right side of his face.

"You were my hero, you son of a bitch! That's for sleeping with my girl. I thought you were so great. You're nothing but a pretty-boy actor. And a sleazeball!" Greg shouted at him.

Sebastian tried to assess what just happened.

Greg had no idea what Sebastian would say back to him. Would he deny it? Would he admit it? Would he make up some lame excuse?

In a quick moment, Sebastian stood up, stepped out from behind his desk and punched Greg in his stomach. "You're the asshole!" he said loudly. "Get the fuck out of my house!"

Lexi heard the commotion and went to the office. When she walked in she couldn't believe what she saw. Sebastian had a big red mark on his cheek and Greg was bent over, coughing and gasping for air.

"Oh my God!" she shrieked. "What happened?"

Greg tried to straighten himself up to regain his dignity. "Come on, Lexi. We're leaving," he told her.

"What are you talking about?"

"Sebastian threw us out!"

Lexi looked at Sebastian quizzically.

"That's not what I said," he explained. "It's time for Greg to leave, but you're welcome to stay, Lexi.

In fact, I'd like you to stay, if you want."

Lexi was frazzled. Was she supposed to choose between her boyfriend and the gorgeous TV star at that instant? She paused to look at them both.

"Forget it! If you don't know what to say, then you've already said it all, you slut!" Greg told her in disgust.

Lexi was shocked that he used that word. She'd never heard him say something like that before.

"Greg?" she called after him as he headed to the front door.

"Good luck with your actor *friend*. Just remember, actors are all professional liars who can't be trusted. Actually, that makes you two perfect for each other!" Greg said as he slammed the door in her face.

Lexi opened the door and ran after him. "Greg, wait! You're being completely unreasonable!"

"Oh, *I'm* behaving badly? Is that what you're saying? I fly all the way out here to celebrate with you just to find out you're screwing James, Sebastian, whatever his name is."

"But I'm not, I didn't–"

"Save it, Lexi. If you haven't yet, then you will. I can see it in your eyes."

"Greg–"

He wouldn't let her get a word in. "You know, you guys just can't treat people like this. There are always consequences for your actions," Greg said in a threatening tone.

"What do you mean by that?" Lexi asked.

"And I used to really like him," he said shaking his head in disappointment.

"I thought you really liked ME," Lexi responded, feeling quite hurt.

Greg turned away from her, pulled out his cell phone and called a cab. Lexi walked back inside Sebastian's house with her feelings all jumbled up.

"Well, I guess you're stuck with me," she told Sebastian. She hoped he would be happy about it, but she wasn't so sure. Was she an imposition? Look at all the trouble she'd created. Since she was supposed to go back to Atlanta the next day, Lexi thought maybe Sebastian would be fine with letting her stay for one more night.

"Or do you want me to go back to the Marriott?" she asked.

Before Sebastian could answer, Lexi looked at his handsome face and saw that it was starting to swell up.

"Let me get you some ice for your face. I'm sorry Greg did that to you. What a jerk!"

"No, I deserved it. He was right. I was making moves on his girlfriend. I would've done the same thing if I was in his shoes. As a matter of fact, that reminds me that I have some unfinished business with my former friend, Tom."

"Leave Tom alone. Hitting people doesn't solve anything," Lexi insisted. "Come into the kitchen and sit down while I get you the ice."

Sebastian did as she instructed and this time Lexi was the one taking care of him. It felt good to both of them.

Chapter 12 – Visitors

Lexi got ready for the big awards banquet that she'd been looking forward to for weeks, ever since she was notified she was one of the contest winners. She'd shopped all over Atlanta to get just the right outfit for the occasion – a sparkly silver and black evening dress with matching accessories and shoes. Wearing those clothes while being in LA made Lexi feel like a glamorous movie star who was going to a big movie premier. She was happy and relaxed which, considering recent events, was quite a feat.

Lexi smiled at Sebastian and said, "I don't know how long this thing will last but I imagine it'll probably take about three hours so I shouldn't be too late. What are you going to do while I'm gone?"

Sebastian looked at Lexi and decided she was stunning, even with her wild colored hair.

"Well, I don't think I'll be going anywhere until

the redness on my cheek goes away. But I'm sure I can find plenty of things around here to keep me busy. You just go and have fun! Make sure to call Sam about twenty minutes before you're ready to leave so he can be there in time to get you."

"Okay, I will. Thanks for everything."

Lexi picked up her clutch purse, checked her lipstick in a wall mirror and headed to the front door.

"Wait!"

Lexi turned around and saw Sebastian trotting towards her.

"What? Did I forget something?"

"Yes!" He put his hands on Lexi's shoulders and pulled her towards him for a gentle kiss goodbye. "Congratulations, beautiful. Enjoy yourself!"

Lexi smiled so big that her dimple expanded to its largest size ever. "Thanks! I will!"

She was practically skipping as she made her way outside where Sam was waiting for her with the car's motor running. When he saw Lexi approaching, Sam stepped out of the car to open the rear door for her. A few moments later, they drove away.

Once Lexi left, Sebastian surveyed the damage to his face. *It's not really that bad,* he thought. He picked up the phone.

"Hey. Why don't you come over? Yeah, now. Let's take care of this," he said. He hung up the phone and went to his room to prepare for his visitor.

About forty minutes later Amanda walked into the foyer. She was five feet, eight inches tall in bare feet, but the Prada stilettos she was wearing had her tipping the six foot mark. Her naturally hazel eyes were turned emerald green thanks to the help of colored contact lenses. And her chestnut brown hair, which was supplemented with many tiers of expensive hair extensions, cascaded below the middle of her back. She was wearing a cleavage–revealing pink ruffled silk blouse, skinny jeans and a diamond bracelet.

"Sebastian, I'm here," Amanda announced.

"Upstairs," he replied.

Sebastian had a whole seduction scene awaiting her arrival – lit aroma therapy candles, soft music, an open bottle of wine. Amanda walked into his bedroom, saw the set-up, and felt ambushed.

"I thought we were going to talk!" she chastised him.

"We are. But we always talk best in bed, don't we? Let's try to hash things out and see if we can reconnect. I'm willing to give you, I mean us, another chance."

Sebastian thought he was being very Parisian about the whole thing considering what Amanda was doing the last time he saw her.

"I told you on the phone already, the only thing I want to discuss is the publicity situation. Let's go down to the living room and talk in there," she insisted.

Sebastian was tired of Amanda having her way.

"No!" he said strongly.

Amanda was not used to being told no, especially from Sebastian who was usually quite accommodating towards her.

"What?"

"You heard me, no!" he repeated. "If you want to talk, we can talk in here. I'm comfortable." He was pissed and was damn-well not going to take orders from her after the way she'd treated him.

"Fine. Let's talk then," Amanda said while standing in the doorway.

"Come in and sit down," he told her, motioning to the bed.

Amanda walked over to the dark gray velvet chair in the corner of the room. She sat with her legs and arms crossed signaling her unwillingness to be there.

Sebastian had the home court advantage. He was sprawled out across his bed wearing nothing but his favorite blue boxer shorts. He'd propped up his back with a few pillows that were pressed against the headboard and his hands were clasped behind his head with his elbows bent on either side of his ears. His legs were crossed at the ankles and he thought he looked calm, yet in charge.

"How could you attack me publicly after what you did to me privately? That was just cruel," he told her while looking into her emotionless eyes.

"I had nothing to do with those press releases, Sebastian, you have to believe me. It was all Kendra's doing. She's a publicity machine, you know that. I guess when she saw that stuff with you and that airplane woman she thought she was doing her job. And she was. That's what she's supposed to do, you know, make me look good in the press," Amanda explained.

"You and I both know that Kendra wouldn't do anything without your go-ahead. Don't try to bullshit me!" Sebastian's face showed his distaste for Amanda's failure to accept any responsibility.

"No, really. Since she couldn't reach me in St. Thomas because my phone was off, she just went for it. And I think she did the right thing. I applaud her initiative," Amanda said coldly.

Sebastian sat up. "You applaud her initiative? You thought she did the right thing? I can't believe what I'm hearing. If you weren't in front of me, I would've sworn that those words didn't come out of your mouth. Did you never love me? Don't you care for me at all?"

"Of course I care about you, but I care more about me. Any other actress in this town would behave the same way. Why should I look like the bad guy to the world?"

He raised his voice. "Because YOU ARE THE BAD GUY IN THIS SITUATION. My God, you're a heartless shrew! How did you hide that side from me for so long?"

"Let's not resort to name calling, Sebastian.

That's low, even for you," she snapped at him.

"What do you mean, 'low, even for me'? You think I'm a lowlife, is that what you're saying? If that's the case then why were you with me?"

"Why do you think?" she asked.

"Well, I thought you loved me the way I loved you."

"Grow up, Sebastian! I loved the press. You and I together were a publicity dream. We're both on hit shows and now everyone in the world knows who we are. This has been good for you too, don't deny it. It's just time that our relationship comes to an end."

Sebastian could no longer easily mask the hurt and anger he felt. He lowered his voice. "So you were using me all this time?"

Amanda responded in a milder tone but her words were just as sharp. "We used each other. You didn't really love me, you just think you did. You're an actor who was playing the part of the loving boyfriend, but you know deep in your heart that you never felt true love for me. Come on."

Sebastian was stunned. He thought he really had loved her, deep in his heart. He felt so foolish. He'd been played. Sebastian turned on his acting muscles and changed his expression to indifference. He refused to give that heartless bitch the satisfaction of seeing how upset she made him.

"Well, I don't think we have anything else to discuss here, Amanda. Just give me my house key and go."

"Here, take it," Amanda said as she walked over to the bed and handed him the key. She walked away and said, "Good luck, Sebastian."

He listened to her footsteps go down the stairs and waited for the front door to close when he yelled, "FUCK YOU!" Then, with all his might, he heaved a pillow across the room, hitting the wall. It barely made a sound.

Sebastian blew out the candles, turned off the music, grabbed the bottle of wine and went downstairs to his bar. He was furious. Without another thought, he resorted to the same method of coping he did the last time Amanda upset him, but this time he was in the privacy of his own home, safe from prying eyes.

"Ahh. Come to papa," Sebastian said as he took a big gulp of scotch. It went down smoothly and he was already feeling better. He walked in his underwear to his refrigerator to find something to shove into his mouth. There was little to choose from since he was expecting to be on vacation in St. Thomas for the week. He saw a jar of pickles and grabbed it. Then he went to his pantry and retrieved a bag of potato chips. They would have to do.

As he began to get drunk, Sebastian contemplated his female relationships. *Why had he been so convinced he was in love with Amanda? Was it just because of the great sex? She was gorgeous, that was for sure, but was he really that superficial?* Sebastian had always considered himself to be a deep person, but maybe all the years living in Hollywood corrupted his Midwestern values. It finally became clear to him that Amanda was an extraordinarily shallow, manipulative, and selfish creature.

When he was with Lexi, he had behaved differently. Being around her made him feel strong, relaxed and comfortable, like the guy he used to be, when he was known as Harvey. He liked how Lexi teased him and called him out on his shit. He enjoyed their witty repartee. He liked her sweetness. He concluded that he had indeed become an asshole, but he didn't have to stay that way. From then on he would be more sincere, less jaded, less superficial. He would rediscover his inner Harvey and find true happiness.

Lexi was having the time of her life at the banquet. She sat at a table with some of the nice people she'd met on the tours. They told her they missed her earlier in the day and wanted to know if she was absent because she was feeling sick or did she play hooky to go off and do something more fun?

"Just taking care of some personal issues," Lexi explained.

Then a man from the table next to hers scooted his chair over and whispered in her ear, "I saw you on TV a little earlier. That was some hot stuff! What are you doing later?"

His inappropriate comment made Lexi feel like

a prostitute, but she was determined not to let that slimy guy ruin her night. After all, she'd gone through a lot just to attend the event. She decided she would simply brush him off and enjoy herself.

"Sorry, meeting with the President later. Will have to catch up with you another time," she quipped with a smile.

"Okay, okay. Just wanted to let you know that you're looking fine."

"Thanks. You look nice too. Have a good night." She turned her head away from him and he moved his chair back to his table.

"What was that all about?" the woman seated next to her asked. "You were on TV? Did they interview all of the contest winners? No one came to get me!"

"No, it was something else. No big deal," Lexi said in an effort to downplay it. Then she artfully changed the subject. "I love your dress. It's such a beautiful fabric. Where'd you get it?" The woman happily told Lexi about all the different stores she went to before she found that particular dress. Diversion successful!

Finally, the time came when all twenty winners were called up to the stage in the front of the room. Lexi walked up proudly when she heard her name announced. She accepted her plaque, posed for some pictures and then returned to the table. Her meal was waiting. Lexi was disappointed to find that it was plain roasted chicken. She thought they could have done something a little nicer with the food, especially since everything else had been first class. But she didn't want to be greedy so she let that thought leave her mind and decided it tasted delicious.

When it looked like the banquet was wrapping up, she pulled out her cell phone and called Sam. "I think I'll be done soon," she told him.

"Okay, miss. I'll meet you outside the front door when you're ready."

Lexi really liked Sam. He was such a sweet man and so reliable. Why couldn't every man be like Sam?

A few minutes later, a woman wearing a Marriott name tag crouched down beside Lexi. "Miss Lincoln?"

"Yes."

"Sorry to interrupt your evening, but I was asked to give you this note immediately." She handed Lexi an envelope then stood up, smiled and said, "Congratulations on your award, by the way."

Lexi thanked her. Then she got up from the table and walked to the side of the room to see what she was given. Lexi loved surprises. She ripped the top of the envelope open and pulled out the small note. It was a surprise, alright, but not a welcome one. As she read it, shivers ran down her spine and her face turned white. Lexi ran to her seat, grabbed her award, the goody bag they gave all the winners, and her purse. She said a quick goodbye to everyone and fled to the lobby.

When Lexi walked outside she was relieved to

find Sam's black car waiting for her. She didn't wait for him to get out and open her door, but instead she jumped right into the back seat and said with a tremendous sense of urgency, "GO!"

They drove off. Lexi looked through the window behind her to see if anyone was following them, but fortunately the coast was clear. Whew! Lexi exhaled. Thankfully it wouldn't be long until she was back with Sebastian. He made her feel safe.

Chapter 13 – Scotch

Matt waited for Sam outside Sebastian's gate. He didn't have a clicker for the gate and Sam didn't have a key to the house, but together they could get inside.

When Sam arrived, Matt hopped into the car and Sam drove them up the driveway to the front of the house.

"Thanks for calling me, Sam. Now, let's find out what's going on," Matt said.

After repeatedly ringing the bell and banging on the front door, Matt used his key and they walked into Sebastian's foyer.

"Sebastian?" they yelled. But there was no response.

"You go over there and I'll look over here," Matt told Sam, pointing in different directions.

Suddenly, Matt heard Sam yell. "He's in here! Come quick!"

Matt ran into the media room and saw Sam standing over Sebastian's body. He was lying face down on the floor in his underwear.

"Oh my God!" Matt exclaimed. "Do you think he's dead?"

"He looks dead. Maybe we should call 911," Sam suggested.

The last thing Matt ever wanted to do in any situation was get the police involved. That always made for a publicity nightmare. So before he had no choice but to call them, Matt reluctantly walked over to Sebastian's body and rolled him over. He saw a huge bruise on Sebastian's face. Then he looked around and noticed broken glass on the floor.

"There must have been quite a struggle," Matt told Sam.

"Ahhhh," Sebastian moaned.

"Thank God, he's not dead," Sam said. He and Matt were incredibly relieved.

"Sebastian? Who did this to you?" Matt asked loudly as he gently shook him.

"Shhhh!" Sebastian said.

"Sebastian! Sebastian!" Matt continued.

"Go away!" he told Matt.

Alcohol fumes wafted up from Sebastian's mouth.

"Are you drunk?" Matt asked.

Sebastian didn't answer.

"Come on, Sam. Let's try to get him onto the sofa."

Even though Sebastian was trim, he was solid muscle and dead weight. Matt lifted Sebastian's head and torso while Sam grabbed a hold of his legs.

"On three," Matt told Sam.

"One...two...three..." and with that, they used their might to lift Sebastian off the floor and carry him over to the nearest couch.

Sebastian slowly opened his eyes and saw them standing over him.

"Hey guys."

"Sebastian, what's going on?" Matt asked.

"It's a party. Want some pickles?" he said.

"Pickles? No, I don't want any pickles," Matt replied.

"I'm going to put on a pot of coffee," Sam said.

"Good idea," Matt agreed. "He's useless like this."

Sebastian closed his eyes again. Matt paced anxiously while waiting for Sam to return with the coffee. In all the years that he'd worked for Sebastian he'd never seen him in a state like this, although many of his other clients behaved this way regularly.

"Here you go," Sam said while putting the cup in Sebastian's hand.

Sebastian opened his eyes and took a sip. "Shit! That's hot! Are you trying to kill me?"

"Just drink it," Matt insisted.

Sebastian took a few more sips of coffee and then looked around.

"What are you guys doing here?" Sebastian asked them.

Finally, a coherent question.

"Did someone break into the house? There's broken glass on the floor and you have a small shiner on your right eye."

"Hey, Matt. Good to see you, man." Sebastian touched his eye. "Yeah, that hurts," he said. "Damn that Greg!"

"Who's Greg?" Matt wanted to know.

"Lexi's boyfriend," Sebastian said.

"He hit you?"

"Yeah, but I had it coming. You should've seen the solid punch I laid on him!" Sebastian boasted.

"You were in a fight?" The publicist side of Matt was once again becoming alarmed.

"Nah. Just a couple of friendly exchanges between guys," Sebastian said calmly. Then he took another sip of coffee. "This is good, did you make it Sam?"

"Yes, sir. Thank you."

"Sebastian, who gives a shit about how the coffee tastes? I want to know what the hell's happening," Matt barked.

"Shhh. Not so loud, man."

"Okay." Matt whispered, "What the hell is going on?"

Sebastian drank a little more coffee and then tried to stand up. His legs gave way and he fell back onto the sofa, spilling some of the coffee onto his bare chest.

"Fuck!"

"Are you okay?" Sam asked. He quickly went into the bathroom that was next to the room and returned with a towel. Sebastian wiped himself dry.

"Can't you guys just leave me alone in my misery, please?" Sebastian begged.

"Did Miss Lexi leave you? Is that why you're so upset?" Sam asked.

"Lexi? Yes, she left me. She went to that teeth gala. All women leave me."

"That's not what I mean. Did the two of you break up?" Sam pressed.

"How could he break up with Lexi?" Matt asked Sam. Matt thought that question was ridiculous. "They weren't dating. She was just a rebound lay."

"Amanda. We broke up!" Sebastian informed them.

"Yeah, Sebastian, we already know that," Matt replied.

"You do?" Sebastian seemed surprised. He looked around the room then turned to Sam and asked, "Where's Lexi?"

"That's what we're trying to find out," Sam explained. "We thought you would know where she was."

"How should I know? You're the one driving her. I need her, Sam. Go get her. What time is it?" Sebastian was a mess, to say the least. And his confusion wasn't helping matters.

"It's after midnight. Lexi called me from the

Marriott at around 10:00 p.m. and asked me to pick her up. When I got there, I waited a while for her in the car before I went inside to look for her. The banquet was over and she was nowhere to be found. I called her phone, but there was no answer. That's when I called you."

"But you didn't answer your phone either," Matt jumped in. "And now we know why. You're hammered!"

"Where's Lexi?" Sebastian looked up at them like a child who'd lost his favorite toy.

"That's what we want you to tell us."

"But I told you I don't know. Hey, maybe she's in her hotel room? She said she might stay there," Sebastian recalled.

"Her hotel room?" Matt asked.

"Yeah, tell him Sam."

"Yes, that's right. I forgot. She'd been staying in room 623."

"Of course. That makes perfect sense. She was tired and decided to stay at the hotel. Mystery solved. Okay, Sam. I think we can leave now and let Sebastian sleep it off."

Sam wasn't satisfied with that conclusion. "Don't you think we should call her room just to make sure? Because she did call me to come pick her up, and then what, you think she just changed her mind?" he asked Matt.

"Women change their minds all the time. It's their thing, right? But if you want to call the hotel, then do it."

"Thank you for calling the Marina Del Rey Marriott. How may I direct your call?

"Room 623 please," Sam asked politely.

"And the guest's name?"

"Miss Lincoln," Sam replied.

"I'm sorry, sir. We have a *do not disturb* on that room. I cannot put your call through. Have a nice night."

"Okay, thank you."

Sam repeated to the others what the operator had just told him.

"She must have hooked up with some guy at the banquet," Matt concluded.

"She left me, too?" Sebastian whined.

"It appears so. I'm sorry," Sam said sympathetically.

The forever insensitive Matt shared some of his wisdom. "Sebastian, women suck. Don't sweat it. You'll find a new, hotter chick tomorrow. Right now you just need to rest. And for God's sake, don't go out and let anyone see you like this!"

"Lexi!" Sebastian whimpered. "How could you leave me? I was so good to you."

"I'm going to get him another cup of coffee," Sam told Matt.

"Can you stay with him a little while? I'm gonna go. He doesn't need me," Matt said.

"Sure, no problem."

Sam was always so kind. He genuinely liked Sebastian, and not just because Sebastian paid him generously. They were both gentle souls which was why watching Sebastian suffer made Sam feel sad.

Sam brought Sebastian several more cups of coffee and even helped him into the bathroom and then back onto the couch. Finally, Sebastian fell asleep. Sam figured it was safe to leave so he went home to sleep, too.

Sebastian didn't awaken until early the next afternoon. His entire body was aching, especially his head and his right eye. He walked into the bathroom next to the media room and saw his reflection in the mirror.

"Holy crap!" he said aloud. "Thank God I don't have to go into work."

Sebastian walked up to his room and took a shower. When he had come out of the shower he noticed Lexi's bag, tucked inside the bathroom closet under the towels. He remembered hiding it there before Amanda came over. *That's odd*, he thought. *How did Lexi get dressed today without her stuff?*

He brushed his teeth and tried to piece things together, which was challenging with his head on fire the way it was. He was mad at himself for getting so drunk again. *It was all Amanda's fault, the bitch!*

As he attempted to think things through, Sebastian came to realize that he needed to see Lexi soon, before she headed back to Atlanta. He really liked her company and he wasn't ready for her to go. He wondered what he could do to persuade her to stay a little longer. Sebastian got dressed and then went down to the kitchen to look for Lexi, but she wasn't there.

"Lexi!" he shouted. "Ow!" *Stop yelling,* he told himself.

Sebastian systematically walked around his house looking for Lexi. He saw broken glass on the floor in his media room and kind of recalled smashing his scotch bottle when it was empty.

"Where is she?" he muttered. Sebastian was confused. He looked at the clock and it said 1:25 p.m. What time was her flight? Sam must know.

"Hey, Sam, it's Sebastian."

"Hello, sir. Are you feeling better today?" Sam asked.

"I feel like shit, thanks for asking."

"Did you find the aspirin I left for you on your bathroom counter?"

"What?" Sebastian asked.

"The aspirin. I put two aspirin on the counter next to your razor. Didn't you see them?"

"When did you do that?"

"Late last night, well, more like early this morning, before I left," Sam said.

"You were here last night?" Sebastian didn't remember Sam being at his house last night except when he took Lexi to the banquet, and even then, he didn't actually see him because he was outside in the car.

"How did you get into my house?"

"Matt met me there with your key. I guess you

don't remember," Sam replied.

"Matt was here too? No, I don't remember. Why did you guys come over?"

"We were worried about you because you didn't answer your phone," Sam explained.

While Sebastian appreciated their concern, he didn't need parents. He could get drunk in his house if he wanted and he shouldn't have to worry about his driver and his publicist invading his privacy.

"Okay, Sam. I'm gonna call Matt. Thanks, I'll look for the aspirins."

Sebastian hung up on Sam and called Matt.

"Hello," Matt said.

"What the hell were you doing at my house last night? Are you my dad now? Can't a guy have a few drinks without it turning into an intervention?" Sebastian said angrily.

"Hold on, Sebastian. What do you remember from last night?" Matt asked.

"I don't remember anything, but I just got off the phone with Sam and he told me that the two of you broke into my house to babysit me! Oh, shit. I forgot to ask Sam about Lexi. That's why I called him. I can't yell at you now, Matt, I have to find out what time Lexi's flight leaves. Gotta call Sam back, sorry."

"WAIT!" Matt snapped. "Can I say something?"

"Yeah, okay, what?"

"The reason we went to your house was because of Lexi."

"What about her?" Sebastian asked. "Where is she, by the way? Do you know? I can't seem to find her."

"She called Sam to pick her up after the event, but when he arrived, she wasn't there," Matt explained. "We're pretty sure she hooked up with another guy because she had the *do not disturb* on her room phone. Sorry, man. I know you liked her."

"She found someone new? Do you think she already left for Atlanta?"

"Yeah. Sam said he thought she was scheduled for a noon flight," Matt answered.

"But she left her stuff."

"What stuff?" Matt asked.

"Her carry-on suitcase with everything in it. Why wouldn't she come back for her bag?" Sebastian was perplexed. "It doesn't make any sense."

"Women don't make any sense. She'll probably call you later and expect you to send it to her, like you're her errand boy," Matt said.

"I don't know what to think. I'm going to take some aspirin and check my messages. Maybe she called me," he told Matt.

"Yeah, okay. Good luck."

"Thanks."

Sebastian hung up the phone and, before checking his voicemail, headed upstairs to his bathroom. Sure enough there were two aspirins waiting for him, just like Sam said. He swallowed them and then pulled out Lexi's bag. Sebastian felt kind of funny rummaging through her stuff, so he only gave a cursory examination of the bag's contents and saw that her clothes, her shoes, her makeup and even her daytime purse were in it. How could she just leave all of that behind?

He decided to call the Marriott himself. Mark, a new employee, answered the phone and was extremely helpful. He listened to Sebastian and then told him he would call him back shortly with more information. And a couple of minutes later he did. Mark told Sebastian that the housekeeping staff said no one slept in room 623 for the last two nights and they found the hotel bill still sitting on the floor by the door.

Sebastian closed his eyes for a moment to try to remember what had happened over the last couple of days. He realized that he was the one who put the *do not disturb* on the hotel room's phone after receiving that unnerving call from The Leech. Suddenly, his eyes shot open. He went to his office computer, looked up the number for Rolling Pines in Fontana, California and made another call.

Chapter 14 – To Call or Not To Call

"I'm sorry sir, but we're not at liberty to give out any information regarding our current or former patients."

"Former?" Sebastian asked.

"Yes, at Rolling Pines we follow strict privacy guidelines. I'm sorry but I cannot be of any further assistance."

"What's your name?"

"Jennifer," the voice on the other end of the call replied.

"Jennifer? That's my sister's name," Sebastian lied. He was an only child. "Jennifer, do you watch the TV show *Crime Days and Nights*?"

"Yes, I've seen it, why?" Jennifer spoke with a cool tone, but she was starting to warm up.

"My name's Sebastian Hawk. I play Detective James Gilbert on the show. Maybe you've seen me?"

"You're Sebastian Hawk? Are you serious?" Jennifer's voice rose an octave.

"Yes, I am."

"How do I know it's you? Say something from the show," she tested him.

Sebastian chose a monologue from one of his favorite episodes and in his best James voice said, "Sergeant Rogers, I believe we've found the murder weapon. It's not the tire iron, like everyone suspected. If you examine the clues and the wounds on the victim, you'll notice that before the car backed up on top of him, the trailer hitch pierced his heart. That was the actual cause of death."

"Oh my God! It IS you!!! Oh, Mr. Hawk. You're so great," she cooed.

"Thanks, Jennifer. I was hoping you could help me out with something. I'm trying to solve a real-life mystery. Maybe you could just bend the rules a tiny bit?" He tried his best to charm her. It worked.

Jennifer's voice got quieter. "What do you need to know, Mr. Hawk?"

"Sebastian."

Jennifer let out a little giggle. "Okay, Sebastian. How can I assist you?"

"I want to find out about Travis Orrington. Can you tell me what you know about him? Maybe even fax or e-mail me his file?"

"Oh, no! I can't send you his file. I would be fired for that, I'm sorry. But let me just see what I can find. Hold on, please, just a second." A few moments went by and then Jennifer returned to the phone. "Here it is. I have his file. What do you want to know?"

"Is he a current patient?"

"Um, let me look. It says here that he checked himself out about two weeks ago," she replied.

Oh shit! Sebastian thought. Why hadn't he called earlier, before he told Lexi to go to the banquet?

"He checked himself out? How can he do that?" Sebastian inquired.

"Oh, this isn't a prison, Sebastian. It's a hospital. If the patients don't want to be here, we can't hold them against their will, unless we have a court order."

"Really? So he wasn't sent there by the courts?"

"No. It says that his mother checked him in because he was exhibiting some unusual behaviors and his doctors thought this would be a good place for him to receive treatment for his condition."

"What kind of behaviors? What's wrong with him?" Sebastian asked. He needed to know how dangerous The Leech truly was.

"His diagnosis is paranoid schizophrenia," Jennifer read.

"Does that means he hears voices?"

"It could manifest in a variety of symptoms such as auditory hallucinations, delusions, anxiety, anger, violence and more."

"And they just let him walk out of there?" Sebastian sounded incensed. He couldn't believe what he was hearing.

"Yeah, I know. It's some pretty scary stuff," Jennifer agreed. "You should see some of the crazies we have here. I'm grateful they're not walking around at the grocery store, I can tell you that. But Mr. Orrington must have been feeling better if he left. Usually they stay willingly. It's a good situation here."

"Does his file say what his particular symptoms are?"

"Let's see. He has some paranoia and also delusions of grandeur."

"What's that mean?"

"People with delusions of grandeur might believe they can fly or even that they're famous, like you are. They hold on to these false beliefs despite evidence to the contrary."

"So he's not actually dangerous?" Sebastian needed to know.

"Well, everyone's different of course, but sometimes these delusions can result in aggression or violence if the person believes they must act in self-defense against those who want to harm them," Jennifer explained.

"Oh!"

"Does that help you, Sebastian?"

"Yes, thank you Jennifer. Is Travis on any medication for that stuff?"

"Yes," she said hurriedly, "but I really have to go now. My boss is coming. Thank you for calling the Rolling Pines Center. Have a healthy day.

Goodbye."

"Goodbye Jennifer. You're a sweetheart," Sebastian told her.

Jennifer hung up the phone.

Damn! He's out! He's got Lexi! And he's completely crazy!

Sebastian didn't know what to do next. Should he call the police? He knew Matt would hate that idea, especially since Sebastian was already in the middle of a publicity storm. A kidnapping story linked to him would only make things worse. But wouldn't that be best for Lexi? She might be on the front page of every paper and then everyone would be looking for her? Yes, that was how to find her!

Sebastian was about to dial 911 when he had second thoughts. What if the publicity turns out to be a bad thing for Lexi? What if The Leech freaks out when he finds out the authorities are after him? He might get violent, like Jennifer said. He could hurt Lexi. Perhaps a sneak attack was the best option.

This was too much for Sebastian to think about alone. He thought about who he could call for help. While he had many so-called friends, there were actually only two people who'd come through for him in recent years – Sam, his driver, and Wayne, his manager. It was sad that his two closest friends were people on his payroll, but Sebastian had never stopped to consider that fact.

Sam and Wayne arrived at Sebastian's home within the hour, neither aware of why they were being summoned. Sebastian just told them he had something urgent to talk with them about. The three of them gathered in the living room and Sebastian brought his friends up to speed.

"Sebastian, this is a really big deal," Wayne said with concern. "From what you've told us, Lexi's been abducted by a delusional man who thinks he and Lexi belong together, right? If someone tries to take her away from him he could become extremely violent. I think we should call the police, don't you?"

"I don't know. What do you think, Sam?" Sebastian asked.

"I like Lexi and I don't want anything to happen to her, which is why I understand your concern about bringing in the police. And truthfully, I don't think Lexi even qualifies as a missing person yet. Doesn't she have to be gone for like, twenty-four hours before they'll even consider her in trouble?"

"That's a good point. Okay, this is what I'm thinking. Why don't we try to get her back ourselves and if we can't find her in a day, then we call the cops. How's that sound?" Sebastian proposed.

"You know you're not actually a real detective, don't you, Sebastian?" Wayne asked him. "Talk about delusional. I think what you're suggesting is insane!"

"Don't hold back to spare my feelings, Wayne. Tell me what you really think," Sebastian said sarcastically.

"Sorry, Sebastian, but there's a woman's life at stake here. Are you sure you want to gamble with her life? Plus, don't statistics show that if someone's been abducted, the first day or two are crucial to finding them alive?"

When Sebastian heard Wayne speak in terms of life and death, he couldn't hold it together any longer. Tears rolled down his cheeks. Sebastian turned his head and discretely wiped his face.

"You've convinced me, Wayne. Let's call the police. It's the right thing to do," Sebastian said. Then, to lighten the mood, he quipped, "You know this is gonna cause Matt to implode!"

Detective Gwendolyn Miller from the LA County missing person's department took the call. Detective Miller was a moderately attractive woman in her late thirties with a thick, solid figure and bright blond hair. As a detective, she had an appreciation for the show *Crime Days and Nights*. As a woman, she had a considerable crush on its star, the handsome Sebastian Hawk. So, even though it was customary for people filing a report to come to her office, in Mr. Hawk's case, Detective Miller readily agreed to go to him.

Traffic delays had her arriving at Sebastian's home about an hour and fifteen minutes later. Wayne and Sam were still there and Matt had come over to participate in the meeting as well.

Detective Miller was escorted into the living

room by Matt, who answered the door. He took the opportunity to tell Detective Miller about the potential damage this could bring to his client, should a media frenzy occur. Sebastian overheard them speaking and, after greeting Detective Miller, made a point of saying that locating Lexi was his first priority.

Sebastian and Sam each told Detective Miller everything they could remember about the last couple of days. She listened to their statements and then called the airport to see if either a Lexi or Mary Lincoln had boarded any flights within the last twenty-four hours. She hadn't.

Detective Miller looked through Lexi's suitcase to see if she could find anything that would suggest Lexi's possible whereabouts. When she was done she said, "Thank you for your help, gentlemen. I can assure you that we will do our best to find Miss Lincoln as soon as possible. Mr. Hawk, your information regarding Travis Orrington was most helpful," she said smiling at Sebastian. "And don't worry. I understand the delicate nature of your situation. We'll try to make sure this doesn't appear connected to you if it can be avoided."

All the men got up to thank her and Sebastian walked Detective Miller to the door. She handed him her card. "Call me Gwen and call me anytime, for anything," she said with a smile and a flip of her hair.

After Gwen left, Matt took the opportunity to speak to everyone. "Look, guys, this is an awful thing we have here, both for Lexi and potentially for Sebastian."

Sebastian interrupted him. "Shut up, Matt! Her life is at stake. So what if my fan base falls off for a little while? This isn't a game and I don't appreciate your attitude."

"All right everyone, let's calm down," Wayne mediated. "We're all here because we want to help. Let's just let the police do their jobs, okay?"

"Okay," Sebastian and Sam said.

"Fine," Matt agreed.

Matt and Wayne left, but Sebastian asked Sam to stay behind to keep him company. What he really wanted, though, was a partner.

Sebastian was determined to save Lexi himself. He was a smart guy and he'd been a TV detective for six years. Surely during that time he'd learned something that could be useful in a situation like this. Plus, he felt guilty for letting this happen to Lexi in the first place. If it wasn't for his fame, The Leech never would have found her. And why didn't he check earlier to make sure Travis was still at Rolling Pines? He was angry with himself for that careless oversight. He had to rescue Lexi...and redeem himself.

Sam went out to pick up some sandwiches for them to eat before their big strategizing pow-wow. They couldn't be expected to think straight on empty stomachs. Besides, Sebastian needed to ingest something other than aspirin, which he was taking regularly to ward off the pain from the pounding his body had taken the day before.

While Sam was out, Sebastian went through Lexi's things once again, this time in hopes of finding clues. But as he sifted through her perfumed clothes, he became distracted. He got caught up in her array of dainty items, particularly her frilly undergarments. Sebastian loved a strong woman who was comfortable with her femininity. Lexi, he discovered, was exactly like that. Even though he never knew what candid comment would fly out of her adorable mouth, Sebastian was happy to learn that she was delicate where it mattered most.

When Sebastian was finally able to pull himself away from Lexi's intimate apparel, he systematically went through her huge purse. He needed information about Lexi that would help him find her, but what he found was not helpful in that capacity. It just confirmed what he'd already learned, that Lexi was a study in opposites. She had several speeding tickets tucked away in a zipped compartment and with them a stack of receipts, including one for ballroom dancing lessons. Ballroom dancing, really? She was a speed demon on the road and a girly-girl in her heart.

When he came up with nothing particularly helpful in his efforts to rescue her, Sebastian realized he should be less concerned with getting to know Lexi and focus more on learning everything he could about The Leech. He went downstairs to his office and got on his computer. He searched for anything that might provide clues as to where The Leech could've taken Lexi or how this nutcase might think.

Sebastian wasn't firing on all cylinders, though, until the food arrived. Thank goodness it didn't take long before Sam returned. He brought roast beef and gorgonzola paninis with grilled onions and a garlic aioli. A hearty, LA-style meal. It was exactly what Sebastian needed.

They ate in Sebastian's office while he filled Sam in on his lack of progress. Sam suggested that they try to locate Lexi through the GPS in her phone, something he'd seen on one of Sebastian's shows.

"That's brilliant," he told Sam. "I remember that episode. But can we do that? I think only the police have access to that stuff. Hopefully that's what they're already doing. What other ideas do you have?"

"Well, we could look for information at the Marriott. Maybe someone there could give us some insight into were she might be."

"Yes, that's it! We need witnesses who can offer clues. Nice one, Sam. You're my Watson! Or maybe you're Sherlock Holmes and I'm *your* Watson? Either way, we make a good team. Let's go to the hotel and see what we can find out."

Chapter 15 – Clues?

"Who is Mark?" Sebastian asked the woman at the front desk of the hotel.

"Mark?" the girl answered back.

"Yes, I called earlier and spoke with a new employee named Mark."

An older woman came over and interrupted. "Hello, Mr. Hawk." Evidently she recognized him. "My name is Mrs. Wheeler. Is there something I may help you with?"

"Yes, thank you. I'm looking for someone named Mark. I don't know his last name, but I spoke with him earlier and he was assisting me with something. Is he available?"

"Joe, please go get Mark. He's in the back on break," she said to another man behind the registration counter.

"Thank you, Mrs. Wheeler," Sebastian said.

In less than one minute a young man appeared

and walked over to Sebastian. "Hello, I'm Mark, Mr. Hawk. How may I help you?"

Sebastian asked Mark to step out from behind the desk and walk with him and Sam. Mark complied. As they walked, Sebastian explained that he was trying to find Ms. Lincoln but, like he'd told him when they spoke on the phone, it was a very secretive thing and he needed his utmost discretion.

"Yes sir, I understand," Mark said.

"Sam, tell him what you told me."

"Mark, you see, Miss Lincoln was attending an event in your smaller ballroom last night. When the event ended, she was expected to come to my car, but she never showed up. We need your help to piece together what happened to her."

"I'd love to help you, but I wasn't here last night."

"Who was here?" Sebastian asked.

"Kimberly."

Sebastian handed Mark a photo of Lexi that he'd printed from the Internet. It wasn't the most flattering picture, to be sure, but it was taken by a paparazzi in the hotel's lobby and it offered a clear shot of her face.

"Can you please take this to Kimberly and ask if she recognizes her? If she does, we'd like to speak with her."

Mark took the paper and went to find Kimberly. Sebastian and Sam sat in the lobby awaiting their return. Fortunately there weren't any paparazzi around.

Mark returned with Kimberly, who was a woman in her early thirties with long reddish hair. She looked very corporate, but the tone of her voice was warm as well as professional.

"Hello. I understand you would like some information about the note that I gave to Ms. Lincoln last night."

"Yes, please!" Sebastian said anxiously.

Kimberly looked into Sebastian's bright blue eyes. She got lost in them for a moment. She knew she wasn't supposed to give out that kind of information, but who was she hurting anyway?

"A tall man came up to the counter and asked me for a notepad and a pen. Then he wrote something down, folded the paper over, and instructed me to give it immediately to Ms. Lexi Lincoln. He tipped me twenty dollars to do it, which I thought was a bit unusual because he didn't look like your typical big spender. He was very stiff, if you know what I mean."

"Did you happen to see the note?" Sebastian asked.

"It popped open as I was putting it into the envelope. All I remember was that the top said, 'Mary, I'm here.' I hope that's helpful," she said, smiling at Sebastian.

Sam piped in. "Miss, can you tell us any more about the man? What did he look like? Did you see the kind of car he had?"

Before he'd spoken, Kimberly didn't even

realize Sam was standing there because she was so
fixated on Sebastian's striking face. Sam was used
to being invisible and he took it in stride. It was
part of his job.

"Like I said, he was tall. He was wearing a
blue shirt with a button-down collar. He had short
brown hair. I couldn't see his car from the desk.
You might want to ask the valet."

Sebastian reached out and shook her hand.
"Thank you so much for all of your help. Truly," he
said very sincerely.

"My pleasure, Mr. Hawk," Kimberly answered,
and then she walked away.

"Mark, can you find out which valets were
working last night during the party, please?"

"Yes, sir. I'll be right back."

Sam returned with two young guys, Larry
and Jose. They were dressed in khaki shorts and
Marriott logo polo shirts.

"Hello. I don't know if Mark mentioned to you
why we're here. We're trying to find out about a car
that may have picked up a woman in a black and
silver dress at about ten-something last night."
Sebastian showed them Lexi's picture. "Do either of
you remember seeing her get into a car?" Sebastian
asked.

"Yes, I saw the lady, but only for a second.
She jumped into the back seat of a car and then it
drove right off," Jose responded.

"You saw her? That's great! What did the car
look like?" Sebastian asked excitedly. He felt like

he'd already cracked the case.

"It was a black sedan. It looked like most hired cars."

This was Sam's territory so he asked, "Jose, do you remember if the car had California plates? How long was it waiting for her?"

"I didn't see the tag, and it wasn't waiting there very long, maybe like ten minutes. But I think it may have been the same car that was parked on the curb across the street earlier in the day."

"It was here earlier in the day? How do you know it was the same car? You just said it looked like every other hired car," Sebastian wanted to know.

"There was thick grey smoke coming out of its tailpipe. Usually those cars are in better repair, but this one must've needed to go into the shop for service," Jose explained.

"You said you think you saw it before?" Sam asked.

"Yeah, I remember that too," Larry added. "He was parked across the street for over an hour and then he just left. He never picked up anyone."

"Really? Is that unusual? Don't hired cars get stood up a lot?" Sebastian asked.

"Not often. And why would he be parked over there instead of waiting in the driveway like all the other cars do? At first I thought it was paparazzi looking for you, Mr. Hawk, but no one ever came out of the car. It was like they were just sitting there watching. Weird."

"That is weird, but very helpful. Thanks guys," Sebastian said while shaking their hands. "Sam, give me a couple of your cards. Please call him if you see that car again or if you think of anything else, okay?" Sebastian handed each of them a twenty dollar bill with Sam's business card.

"Thanks. We'll let you know if anything else happens."

Mark was there for the whole exchange. Sebastian turned to him and said, "Mark, you've been extremely helpful. Thanks for everything." Sebastian reached into his pocket and pulled out some money. He peeled off five twenty dollar bills for Mark and another twenty that he asked him to give to Kimberly.

Sam and Sebastian left the hotel and headed over to the police department to speak with Detective Miller.

When they arrived at the police station, Sebastian and Sam were directed to Detective Miller's office. It was on the second floor, the last office on the left.

"Hello, gentlemen, please come in," Detective Miller greeted them. She stood up and shook their hands, and then offered them seats in the two tan chairs in front of her desk.

"How're things going with your investigation, Detective Miller?" Sebastian asked.

She looked at him and said, "Please call me

Gwen."

"Yes, sorry, Gwen," he said with an eager smile. He needed to hear about all of the progress she'd made. Surely, they must have been close to finding Lexi.

Unfortunately, Gwen didn't tell Sebastian what he wanted to hear. "It hasn't been very long so we're really just filling out paperwork and getting everything into the system," she explained.

Sebastian was very upset. He went on a tirade in his head and then got bogged down with other thoughts. *How dare they be so bureaucratic when the woman I love is missing? Oh my God, did I just say that to myself? The woman I love? What's wrong with me? I was just put through the ringer by a she-devil so how could I even have a thought like that? Maybe Wayne's right, I am insane. Should I call Jennifer at Rolling Pines and have her hold open a place for me? No, no, don't be so dramatic, Sebastian. It's like Matt said, I'm on the rebound, that's all. Now I'm agreeing with Matt? There's another problem. But he's right, I can't be in love with anyone right now, especially someone I just met! But I do really like Lexi. She's so damn cute… and she keeps me on my toes and –*

Sam interrupted Sebastian's daydream by speaking. "Gwen, we just came from the Marriott Hotel and we have a bit of information that we hope you'll find helpful."

Gwen took notes as they gave her the description of The Leech. Then they told her that thick smoke was coming out of his car and he appeared to be staking out the place earlier in the afternoon.

"Gwen," Sebastian said with a look of desperation on his face. "When do you think things will start happening? What if he's done something terrible to her? We have to find her immediately! Have you tried yet to locate her by her cell phone's GPS?"

"Mr. Hawk, I understand your concern, believe me I do. I deal with cases like these every day. We will do everything we can to locate Ms. Lincoln. But please be aware that there is no solid evidence indicating any kind of foul play. As of now she's just a missing person, and it's not even been twenty-four hours yet. Should this turn out to be a kidnapping case, then we'll turn it over to the FBI."

"What do you mean no evidence of foul play?" Sebastian was frustrated but tried to speak calmly. "I told you she didn't show up for the car she ordered, she left her suitcase behind, and then the lady at the hotel said a man sent her a note that was addressed to Mary, the name her stalker calls her."

"Yes, but you also told me that the valet said she got into a car of her own free will. Don't you think it's possible that she may have gone off with a friend? Or maybe she got back together with Greg, her boyfriend? Look, you hardly know this woman. She could be anywhere doing anything. Maybe she likes it here so much that she simply stashed her stuff at your place while she went to Disneyland," Gwen said matter-of-factly. "It happens."

"Disneyland? She's not at Disneyland!" Sebastian got more animated. Then he pulled himself together because he didn't want to piss off Gwen. He needed her to work harder. Sebastian looked into her eyes in hopes of connecting with her.

"Gwen, I hear what you're saying, but there is no way that Lexi is just out having fun. She's a reliable person and she's in real trouble, I know it! I'd really appreciate it if you could make Lexi's case a priority. I'll be forever grateful."

Gwen had dealt with celebrities before but none as charming or irresistible as Sebastian.

"I'll do everything I can. I promise," she told him.

"Thank you. Please let us know the minute you have some news." Sebastian stood up and Sam followed his lead. They shook Gwen's hand goodbye and then walked back to Sam's car.

"That was a crock of shit!" Sebastian said in disgust.

"Yes, I agree," Sam said.

Sebastian expressed his thoughts aloud. "How dare she say Lexi's back with Greg? She wouldn't do that, would she? No, I can't imagine it. And even if she did, why didn't she call to tell me. Because she was too ashamed? No, Lexi doesn't get ashamed. She's very forthright. Besides, The Leech has reappeared. It HAS to be him that has her. Maybe the note Kimberly gave her said if you don't get into my car quietly, I'll kill you. Oh my God, Sam. We have to solve this, and fast."

"I'm with you!" Sam responded.

"Great. It's getting dark out. Let's go back to my house and hit the computer again. There's gotta be something we're overlooking."

When they returned home, Sebastian heard his cell phone going off in the kitchen. Had he forgotten to take his phone with him? He never did that before, but without an assistant around to remind him of things, and considering all the stress he was under, it was no surprise he made the oversight. Sebastian ran to grab it.

"Hello?" he said.

"She's mine!" the voice told him.

"Who's yours? Who is this?"

"Stay away from Mary. She's mine," the voice repeated, and then he hung up.

"SAM!!!" Sebastian screamed. "It was The Leech! On the phone!"

"Perhaps you should call Gwen," Sam advised.

"What's she going to do? Type it into her report? Or tell me that it was Greg rubbing my face in the fact that Lexi chose him? No way. I'm not calling her, not yet. Let's get more evidence before we tell Gwen. Let me see if there's a phone number in my caller ID."

Of course there was no number on his phone, it simply said, 'private number.' Nothing was ever that simple and Sebastian knew it. But he also knew this guy wasn't playing with a full deck so he figured anything was possible.

When Sebastian looked at his phone he saw that he'd missed many calls and had several messages. He scanned through them to see if there was anything important, and there it was.

"I've got a text from Lexi!" Sebastian announced to Sam. He held his breath as he hit the button to read it.

"Having a great time @ the banquet. Hope you're having a good night. C U soon. ☺ Lexi"

"What time did that come in?" Sam asked.

"Let's see. It says 9:32 p.m. last night." Sebastian was disappointed.

"Maybe there are more," Sam suggested.

"Let me check. YES! Look! There's one from TODAY!!!"

"Really? Oh, thank heaven!" Sam was relieved. She was alive.

"I'm okay. In small apt. Not too far. GTG"

"What's that mean, 'GTG'?" Sam asked.

"Got to go. She must have sneaked the text. At least she's okay!" Sebastian said. He exhaled.

"Now we have solid evidence that she's been taken. Let's tell Gwen," Sam said.

"That's not evidence that she's being held, is it? She simply said she's okay but had to go. It doesn't exactly say she's in trouble. Gwen won't take it seriously."

But Sebastian felt a huge ton of bricks lift from

his shoulders when he read it. He looked to see what time the text was sent and it was from five hours earlier. He figured that since The Leech had just called him to brag that he had Lexi, she must still be okay.

"Now we just have to find a small apartment suitable for a leech!" he said to Sam.

Chapter 16 – Gwen

Nothing good ever comes from making rash decisions. That was a lesson Lexi Lincoln had a hard time learning. Before kissing Sebastian in the airplane – which, let's face it, caused both of them endless problems – her last impulsive act was purchasing ballroom dancing classes. She'd paid for fifteen lessons even though she only attended two, after discovering that she was the youngest person there by at least twenty years. Yet, she did go to two because Lexi didn't believe in giving up on anything after only one chance.

Think before you act. That's what Lexi needed to work on. But who could really blame her for panicking when she received the note at the banquet that read, 'Mary, I'm here and I'm coming to get you right now'? By assuming that the black sedan in the driveway belonged to Sam, she created the situation she feared most, losing control.

It wasn't until she was in the car for nearly an hour that Lexi realized Sam wasn't driving. She had sat in silence, spreading her thoughts between feeling proud of herself for receiving an award and fearing that The Leech would once again take over her life.

And now, there she was, a prisoner in a small apartment somewhere in California. She was so mad at herself for not being more careful. And she was determined to get out of there in one piece, even though she had no idea how she would do it.

Her captor gave her a pair of shorts and a t-shirt to wear so she would better blend in. She was more comfortable in them too, but that wasn't his goal. He had other plans for Lexi, which is what she feared. She had no idea what those were and she chose not to allow herself to get carried away with scary thoughts. She decided she would simply focus on how to escape.

Lexi watched him put her cell phone in the cabinet in the bathroom. It was a stupid move on his part. *Why not just throw it away? No one ever said kidnappers were rocket scientists*, she figured. She spent the night trying to devise a way to unlock the door to her room and make her way to the phone. Getting to her phone was her best shot at getting help. She got there once, when she told him she needed to use the bathroom, but then he walked by and she had to get it back inside the cabinet before he caught on.

The room she was kept in was small and plain. It was painted peach and the only piece of furniture in it was a mattress on the beige carpeted floor. There was a window facing the woods and one light that was attached to the ceiling. Since the apartment was on the fourth floor of the building, jumping out the window didn't seem prudent. If she could just get out of the room somehow, she knew she'd have weapons at her disposal. She would have to think of something that would help her make her way to safety.

She could hear him in the other room, watching television and typing onto his computer's keyboard. He was a big fan of the Internet. She even heard him on the phone a couple of times, but she couldn't make out what he was saying. Damn!

All Lexi was sure of was that this guy was dangerous. She didn't know how long she had before he wanted something from her that she was not prepared to give. That fear motivated her to keep coming up with plans until something made sense, until she knew her idea would definitely work. She would not be rash. Not ever again.

Sebastian and Sam were up until the wee hours of the morning trying to find Lexi. At first Sebastian theorized that The Leech would take Lexi to Las Vegas to make her his wife because The Leech was insistent that they belonged together. But it was a long shot and fairly unlikely that The Leech would take her to such a crowded, public place. Sam agreed and they scratched that idea off the list.

Eventually Sebastian thought of searching the government real estate tax records to see if Travis Orrington owned any property. Bingo! A small piece of land not far from the California/Nevada border. That must be where he's holding Lexi, Sebastian concluded.

"Do you think we should tell Gwen?" Sebastian asked Sam.

"I don't know. Do you think she'll finally do something once she gets the information?" Sam answered.

"Yeah, that's the magic question, isn't it? I guess we'll have no way of knowing unless we tell her."

Sebastian was brave, but he wasn't stupid. Even though he'd spent hours researching Travis Orrington, he was smart enough to realize that he had no idea what he was really up against with this guy. He needed professionals to deal with The Leech when the time came for physically subduing him.

Sebastian offered Sam the guest room and he went up to his bedroom to get some sleep. He hoped the morning would provide a fresh perspective.

Sebastian was startled when he walked into his room. There, spread out across his bed, were all of Lexi's things. He was surprised by and unprepared for the emotional reaction that followed. His breath caught in his throat and terrible thoughts ran through his mind. What if she was dead? How would he live with that guilt? Or worse yet, what if he never found out what happened to her? The not knowing, he had heard, was the worst thing imaginable, though he wasn't so sure he agreed with that statement.

He moved Lexi's things to *her side* of the bed and then he got undressed and went to sleep.

Sebastian awoke at 6:30 a.m., when he heard the faint sound of a bird chirping outside his window. Even though he'd only had three hours of sleep, the adrenaline running through him made him feel invigorated and ready to take on The Leech. As he showered, he thought about what kind of clothes to put on. *What would his character, Detective James Gilbert, wear?* Sebastian dressed in what he considered appropriate investigative gear and then went into the guest room to wake Sam.

After breakfast they called Gwen. She wasn't in her office yet so Sebastian called her on her cell.

"Detective Miller," she answered.

"Hi Gwen. It's Sebastian, Sebastian Hawk. How are you this morning?" He thought a little sweet talk couldn't hurt, especially since she wasn't a believer in the whole kidnapping thing and he needed her to come on board.

"Good morning, Mr. Hawk. What can I do for you?"

"I'd like to talk with you in person. Do you have time to meet with me soon?" he asked.

"I work the late shift so I don't get into the office until the afternoon. However, I'm going to be in your neighborhood later this morning. If you like, I can meet you somewhere or I can come to your house."

Gwen saw that as her opportunity to make a move on Sebastian. She'd been divorced for four months and dating a celebrity would be doubly good because it provided the added bonus of pissing off her ex-husband.

"I'd prefer if you came to the house, because of the paparazzi situation," he told her. "If they see me speaking with a detective or if someone overhears us, then the cat's out of the bag, right?"

"Yes, I see your point," she happily agreed. "I'll be over in about an hour and a half. Okay?"

"Great. I can't wait," Sebastian replied.

He suspected that Gwen might have a thing for him. Most women did. Lexi was the only woman he'd met in recent years who was completely unfazed by his celebrity. That was partly what made her so damn attractive to him.

Sebastian didn't forget the painful lesson he learned from Amanda – as a rule, women have ulterior motives. Well, he figured, two could play at that game. He was not adverse to using his celebrity status to help him get what he wanted from Gwen, just as he did with Jennifer from Rolling Pines.

"Hello Sam, I didn't expect to see you here," Gwen said as she walked into Sebastian's living room.

"Good morning, Detective," Sam replied.

"So, Mr. Hawk, may I call you Sebastian?"

"Oh, I insist," he said with a smile.

Gwen smiled back. "Sebastian, you asked me to come over. What's going on?"

Sebastian filled Gwen in on all of the developments since their last meeting. He told her about The Leech's phone call, he showed her Lexi's texts and then he showed her a print out of the tax rolls with Travis Orrington's information. He even produced a map where he had circled the area where The Leech's property is located.

"Sebastian. Sam. You men are very impressive. I think maybe I should be concerned for my job. You're not after it are you?" she said teasingly.

"Do you think there's enough here to call in the FBI?" Sebastian asked directly.

Gwen stood up and walked over closer to the map, closer to Sebastian. She bent over it revealing the trim on her lacy bra and her ample cleavage. Her straight blond hair hung down onto the map and she carefully moved it out of the way, making sure Sebastian took notice.

"Well, based on what I see, you've done a lot of solid homework. The text from last night indicates that Lexi intended to see you shortly and the next one could have been her attempting to alert you to her whereabouts." Gwen stood up and turned around to look Sebastian in his eyes. "You get an A+. Let's call the feds!"

That was the answer they wanted to hear. Sebastian picked Gwen up and whirled her around. That was the reaction she wanted to get. Everyone was happy, even Sam, who sat quietly in his chair watching the whole production.

Gwen pulled out her cell phone and called her supervisor. She informed him of the new developments and got the go-ahead to call the FBI. She spoke with her contact there, Agent Roman Young. He was a smart, balding middle-aged man with a serious demeanor and a reputation for getting things done.

"Hi Roman. How's it going over there today?" Gwen asked.

"Hi Gwen. It's not too bad. You?"

"Well, I've got a new case for you. Do you have any time this morning to come to the Hollywood Hills area?" she asked him.

"Sure. I'm not far from there now. Text me the address and I'll head over. Will you wait for me?"

"Of course."

Agent Roman liked Detective Miller. After learning of her recent divorce, he was hoping to take her out, on the side. His wife traveled a lot and so did he, which made it easy to hide his affairs. Plus, in his business, he knew how to keep things quiet.

As far as Sebastian was concerned, Gwen had already served her purpose so he left her to chat with Sam in the living room while he went back to his office. That's when his cell phone rang.

"How much is Mary worth to you?"

"What?" Sebastian was caught off guard. He should have thought when it said 'private number' that it could have been The Leech, but all celebrities have unlisted phones that show up as 'private number' so he didn't think twice when it rang. However, once he heard the word Mary, he dashed into the living room, but it was too late. The call had ended.

"What happened?" Sam asked as Sebastian flew into the room.

"It was HIM! I can't believe you were here, Gwen, and you didn't get to hear him." Sebastian was frustrated.

"What did he say?" she asked.

"He wanted to know how much Mary was worth to me. Does that mean he wants a ransom?"

"It sure sounds like it," Gwen said. "And now we have a motive, and a definite kidnapping scenario."

Sebastian felt vindicated, but that feeling left him immediately. He was upset that he didn't say something better than "what". There was his opportunity to gather real clues and he blew it. James Gilbert never would have made that mistake.

Gwen could see the concern on Sebastian's face.

"This is good news Sebastian. The more he

contacts you the better chance we have of nabbing him and finding her alive."

There was that word again, alive. Why did people keep saying that? Sebastian knew what was at stake and he didn't like being reminded time and time again that Lexi could be hurt.

The buzzer for the gate finally sounded. Agent Roman had arrived.

Chapter 17 – FBI

Sebastian looked at his cell phone and saw that it was Matt on the line. He pushed the 'ignore' button and returned his attention to Agent Young. Then the phone rang again.

"I'm sorry, but I have to take this. I'll be right back," he said as he walked out of the room.

"Matt. What's up? I'm kind of in the middle of something right now."

"Yeah, you kind of are! Turn on your TV, channel 8, now!" Matt insisted.

Sebastian went into his media room and did as Matt instructed.

"Son of a bitch!" he exclaimed. He couldn't believe his eyes. There on a talk show was Patty the flight attendant. She appeared to be going on and on about the inappropriateness of public displays of affection. And seated next to her was none other than Greg!

"But...how...I..." Sebastian stumbled for the right words.

"My thoughts exactly," Matt said.

"What the hell is this?" Sebastian asked.

"I believe it's called a public flogging," Matt undiplomatically replied.

"You have got to be shitting me." Sebastian stood there with his eyes and ears fixated on his TV. He truly couldn't believe the ridiculousness of the whole thing, the sheer spectacle of nonsense.

"So what does this mean?" Sebastian asked Matt.

"You know, Sebastian, I honestly have no idea."

The fact that Matt was stumped freaked Sebastian out even more. Matt was always a bit arrogant, but that's why Sebastian had such faith in him. He was a bulldog who was ready and able to get any job done.

"Okay, well, as much fun as it is to watch this, I have the FBI in the other room so I guess I have to leave you to clean up this mess on your own," Sebastian told him.

"What do you mean you have the FBI in the other room? When were you going to tell me? Sebastian, that's HUGE. I need to know these things."

"Detective Miller called some guy named Agent Young from the FBI to find Lexi. They're finally agreeing that she's been kidnapped. Can you believe it took them so long?"

"I can't believe any of what's been happening.

I'm on my way over," Matt told him.

"Why?"

"I need to be there. See you in a little while."

Sebastian hung up the phone and, after another moment of staring at the TV, turned it off and headed back to the living room to continue his meeting. That's when the gate buzzed.

"Who the hell is it now?" Sebastian mumbled to himself.

"Mr. Hawk. I'm here."

It was Margarit, his housekeeper. He buzzed her in and then he finally walked back into the living room.

"Sebastian, Miss Lincoln told you that she had a restraining order against Travis Orrington two years ago, correct?" Agent Young Asked.

"Yes that's right," Sebastian answered.

"And then you said that when you were in her hotel room he called your cell phone and her hotel phone. Miss Lincoln verified that it was indeed Travis' voice on the messages."

"Yes, she did," Sebastian responded.

"Then, the night of the banquet, you believe Miss Lincoln received a written note from him with some kind of threat that caused her to get into a car with him."

"Exactly."

"May I see her things? Detective Miller said you have them upstairs."

"Of course," Sebastian told Agent Young.

Sebastian, Sam, Gwen and Agent Young all

went up to Sebastian's room. After giving Lexi's belongings a quick review, Agent Young gathered them into her bag and carried it downstairs into the living room.

"I'm going to do a bit of research and see what I come up with," Agent Young told everyone. "Do you have any questions for me?"

"How long does your process take? I mean, do you expect to start looking for Lexi today or do you have other priorities that'll push her to the back of the line?" Sebastian wanted to know.

"This is now my first priority. I will probably call you later with some more questions. Do I have all of your contact information correct?"

Agent Young showed Sebastian and Sam his notes and they nodded in agreement.

"What if he calls again? Don't you want to tap my phone so you guys can trace the calls?" Sebastian asked.

"We can get recordings from your phone carrier, but most likely he's using a disposable mobile phone which is nearly impossible to trace," Agent Young explained. "Anything else?"

Sebastian looked at Sam who shook his head no.

"I guess not right now," Sebastian replied.

"I'll be in touch," Agent Young said. "Detective Miller, I'll be happy to walk you to your car."

They left and then Sebastian turned to Sam, "I guess you can go home now. I can't thank you enough for all of your help."

"You don't have to thank me. I just want them to find Miss Lincoln."

"You and me both, man."

"Call me if you need me for anything," Sam said. And Sebastian knew he meant it.

"I will. Have a good one."

Sebastian changed into his shorts to prepare for a good run. However, when he stepped outside his house, there were several reporters standing outside his gate eager to ask him important questions.

"Mr. Hawk, what do you think about public displays of affection? Do you think you and Ms. Lincoln went too far on the airplane?"

Sebastian quickly turned around and went back inside. He was a prisoner in his own home. This was new for Sebastian who had never been a publicity hound. He liked being an actor simply because he loved the craft of acting. It wasn't until he began dating Amanda that the paparazzi started taking notice of him. Sure, as she pointed out, it was good for his career. His pay was based loosely on his fan base and the more they saw of him, the more of them there were. But he hated that part of the job. He would rather make less money and have more privacy, at least that's what he told himself.

Sebastian was all dressed up with no place to go, so he went back to his office. He hadn't checked the Internet for a while and he was sure it had more bad news waiting for him. Unfortunately, he was right.

Not only were video clips from that stupid talk show all over the gossip sites, but he saw more postings from The Leech. It was the same thing as before. 'Stay away from Mary. She's mine.' Why was he still doing that when he already had her? What more could he want, except for Sebastian's money, of course?

Sebastian checked several sites and it was the same thing everywhere, over and over again. Sebastian began to wonder what would happen if he posted something too? Sebastian could hide behind a dumb, anonymous username, like everyone else did. What would he call himself, he pondered. He knew it had to be something that people would never figure out was him, unlike The Leech whose username was the less imaginative: travisorr12345. Maybe Sebastian could use a woman's name or a word that's not even a word?

'Mary is never going to be yours,' he wrote under the pseudonym udontknowjack28. He liked the message that the words in his username conveyed, and the "28" was simply his age, so why not? He went to as many sites as he could find and wrote his message. Fight fire with fire, that's what Matt taught him. And with that thought lingering in his mind, the gate buzzed. It was Matt.

"Hey, man," Sebastian said when he opened his front door.

"Do you see what's going on outside?" Matt asked.

"Yeah, I tried to go for a run and ended up running right back into my house."

"I'm so sorry, Sebastian. I feel like I really lost control of this thing. I don't know what I could have done to prevent it, but I should have somehow found out about the talk show ahead of time. I dropped the ball. My bad," Matt apologized.

"Don't sweat it. How could you know? How could anyone know? This thing has taken on a life of its own," Sebastian said in disgust. "Whatever the fall-out is, so be it. All I care about right now is Lexi. Let me show you what I just did on the web."

Matt didn't think it was a good idea to be responding to The Leech, but he didn't think it was a bad idea either. The fact of the matter was that neither of the men knew what to do.

"Maybe you should speak to the FBI guy before you start interacting with that psycho," Matt said.

"Fucking with The Leech over the Internet gives me a tiny bit of satisfaction. It doesn't actually change things, I know that."

"I'm just saying you don't want to do anything to make matters worse," Matt said out of concern for Lexi.

"No, of course not. Come to think of it, Matt, how do you feel about taking a long drive?"

"Where to?" Matt asked.

"I'm thinking somewhere near the Nevada border. That's where The Leech's place is,"

Sebastian told him.

"Sebastian, we're not cops. Let them do their thing and you stay here and be safe. Look at your beat-up face. You're already screwing with your product. If you get shot or stabbed or blown up, then what?"

Sebastian laughed. "Matt, your sensitivity is touching."

"What?" Matt was being serious.

"I'm not saying we should take him down, I just want to see if we can find the place. I don't have any big plans to go in and rescue Lexi by myself. Okay?"

Matt looked at Sebastian and he didn't believe a word he was saying about not wanting to rescue this girl. He knew Sebastian and he knew that was exactly what he was thinking of doing, which is why Matt decided he'd better go with him – to prevent him from doing something stupid, or worse yet, dangerous.

Chapter 18 – Information

Lexi heard him approaching her door. *Should I try to overtake him?* she wondered. She had been taking kickboxing lessons for the last six months and had some good power in her small body. But what would happen if it backfired and all she did was make him mad, like poking a bear? She wouldn't act rashly, that was the mantra she kept repeating in her head. *Wait 'til I have a solid plan,* she told herself.

He opened the door to her room and handed her a sandwich. It was a fancy sandwich on a plate, which surprised her. She expected something like a cheap bologna sandwich, but instead it was a beautiful baguette filled with chicken salad that had grapes and nuts in it. He went into her room to watch her eat. She looked up at him from time to time only to see him staring at her. What was he thinking? Then he spoke.

"Are you enjoying that?"

"Uhuh, thank you," she responded with one of her signature smiles. "Aren't you going to have something to eat, too?" she asked him.

"I already ate, thanks."

"Oh, well, it's good. I appreciate it."

It was the strangest conversation she'd ever had. She didn't know what to do, so kill him with kindness was the approach she went with.

"You look nice in that shirt. It suits you," she told her captor.

He looked down at his shirt to see what he was wearing.

"Really, you like this? I always thought it was baggy in weird places."

"No, not at all. It makes you look quite handsome," she said trying to sound sincere even though she was actually scared out of her mind.

"Well, thanks. I think those ugly clothes I gave you actually look good on you. Now that dress you were wearing last night, wow! That was beautiful, but not practical for what we have to do," he told her.

"What do we have to do?" she asked without hesitation. Lexi needed information.

"Don't worry about it. Just eat your lunch. Do you want something to drink? I've got water or Coke."

"Water, please." Lexi chose water because if he wanted to put a drug or something inside the Coke, she wouldn't be able to see it or taste it like she could with water. This way, she figured, she would at least have some idea as to what she was ingesting. Of course that logic didn't make any sense since she had just eaten a sandwich that could have been laced with any number of poisons.

"I'll be right back. Don't do anything stupid. I still have that big knife."

"I'll stay here," she assured him.

He returned shortly with her drink and Lexi thought since they were getting on so well that she would ask him for a little more latitude.

"It's kind of boring in here all by myself. Do you think maybe I could watch TV out there with you?"

"I'll get you a magazine," he said. "I don't want you leaving me, if that's what you're thinking."

"No, not at all. I just thought it would be nice to spend some time talking with you or getting caught up on some shows. Do you have any favorite programs? I love the reality shows. Have you ever seen *Iron Chef*? It's great!" Lexi smiled and tried desperately to get through to his humanity.

"Maybe later. Just relax for a while and I'll look around for something you can read."

"Okay. Thanks."

He took her plate and her glass and then left the room. She heard him lock her door from the other side.

Progress, she thought.

Sebastian changed out of his running clothes back

into his version of detective garb and was about to grab his car keys when his phone rang.

"Hello," Sebastian answered.

"Hello, Mr. Hawk. I was going over things and I was wondering if you could come to my office so we could talk a bit more?" Agent Young asked.

"Absolutely. I'll come right over," Sebastian agreed.

"Thanks. See you soon."

Sebastian and Matt drove to the FBI headquarters for the Los Angeles area. Sebastian thought it was strange that he hadn't gone there when he was doing research for his television role. It was an oversight that he would now make up for, even though that wasn't his current priority.

Sebastian found Agent Young's office on the 9th floor of the government building. He had a large metal desk with a map of LA on the wall behind him and two blue chairs on rollers in front of his desk.

"This is my publicist, Matt Walker," Sebastian said as means of introduction.

"You didn't have to bring a publicist with you, Mr. Hawk. At the FBI, we're very careful to keep things close to the vest, as the saying goes."

"Oh, he's not here as my publicist, just as a friend. Matt was at my house when you called so he decided to come along. I hope that's okay," Sebastian explained.

"No problem. Let's get started then." Agent Young was all business and Sebastian was too, as far as this matter was concerned. He knew they would get along great.

"What do you want me to tell you?"

"Do you know anything about Miss Lincoln's family?" Agent Young asked.

"Why does that matter?" Sebastian asked politely. "I thought this was about finding him, Travis, The Leech."

"It's about learning as much as we can about both of them so we are best prepared to rescue her," Agent Young explained.

Sebastian couldn't argue with that.

"I know that her parents aren't together any more. She speaks to her mom a lot. In fact, her mother contacted her after she saw the airplane video of us."

"What do you know about her father?" Agent Young asked.

"Nothing really. Why?"

"Miss Lincoln's father has a criminal record. He's been out on parole for the last few months. Do you know if she's had any contact with him?"

"No. Sorry. She never mentioned him."

Sebastian was shocked to hear that Lexi had criminals in her family. It made him realize that he didn't know her as well as he thought he did.

"How about her siblings? Did she tell you about them?"

"Um, yeah. She said that she has a twin brother in grad school and a younger, half-sister who's in tenth grade," Sebastian said.

"Her brother, Jerry, has a history of gambling. What can you tell me about that?"

"Nothing, sorry."

"Okay. What about this Greg guy – her boyfriend. What's his story? He hit you. Would you say he has a hot temper?"

Sebastian didn't know how to answer that. *On the one hand*, he thought, *yeah, the guy's a total asshole.* But on the other hand, he knew that the attack was justified.

"He's an accountant in Atlanta. I don't know if I would call it a hot temper exactly. I mean, the guy flew across the country to be supportive of his girlfriend's accomplishment and then found her staying with another man. Even though there was nothing major going on between us, it looked pretty bad. I guess I really don't blame him for behaving the way he did, do you?"

Agent Young continued. "When he found you two together, did he make any threats?"

"No. At first he was excited to meet me because he's a fan of my show. But then, out of nowhere, he marched into my office and hit me, so I threw him out of my house. It was the night Lexi disappeared. Do you think Greg's a factor in all of this? He didn't seem to know anything about The Leech until we told him. Plus, he was the one who called Travis' mom and found out about Rolling Pines. Could he have been pretending? Do you think he and The Leech are somehow connected?"

"I'm not drawing any conclusions just yet,

Mr. Hawk. Please allow me to gather more information."

"Fine."

"What about the people she's living with? What do you know about them?" Agent Young probed.

"Um, Lexi mentioned that her landlord called her to say she saw her on the Internet. I know they don't have a lot of money which is why they rent a room to Lexi. Do you think *they* put The Leech up to this? Is that what you're getting at?"

"Again, I know you want to solve this and so do I, but it's too soon to draw any conclusions. I just want to collect all of the information I can," Agent Young explained to Sebastian.

Matt was sitting there listening and he couldn't believe all the craziness that was connected to Lexi. A convict dad? A gambler brother? Renting a room, who does that?

"Did Mary talk to you at all about her boss, Dr. Weinstein?" Agent Young continued.

"She thought very highly of him and of all the people in her office," Sebastian answered. "She had a good relationship with them as far as I know."

"Now, let's get to Travis Orrington."

"Good."

"You said that she went on just three dates with him. During their last date at Red Lobster, Miss Lincoln told him she didn't want to see him any more. He became agitated and told her that they were meant for each other, right?"

"Yeah. She said he went wild in the restaurant

and said that he would do whatever it took to prove to her that he was the man for her," Sebastian reiterated.

"After that she got many notes from him saying how much he cared about her. One was very threatening, however, and that prompted her to go to the police," Agent Young read from his notes.

"Uhuh."

"But he kept pursuing her in spite of the restraining order against him so eventually she changed her name and moved to another state?"

"Yes. That's correct," Sebastian agreed.

"Tell me about Rolling Pines. You spoke with one of their employees on the phone who told you that Mr. Orrington was a patient there up until two weeks ago."

"Yes," Sebastian answered.

"How did you obtain that information, Mr. Hawk? That's not something they would legally be able to share with you. Also, you claim you were told of Mr. Orrington's diagnosis and symptoms? That seems highly unlikely," Agent Young said skeptically.

"Are you accusing Sebastian of something?" Matt spoke up.

"No, I'm simply asking him to explain how he came to gather such confidential information," Agent Young replied.

"I have a way with women, okay?" Sebastian told him.

"What? Did you say that you have a way with

women?" The look on Agent Young's face was priceless. It was a combination of disbelief and envy.

"Yeah. I spoke with a woman on the phone and when she found out I was from a TV show, she became very helpful. It's a perk of my job." Sebastian tried to sound humble even though he knew being a celebrity gave him clout.

"This way you have with women, would you say it worked on Patty Parker?" Agent Young asked.

"Who?"

"The flight attendant," Matt interjected.

That's her name? Patty Parker? Ha! She sounds like a cartoon character, Sebastian thought. But he didn't dare say it aloud. They were having a serious conversation.

"Oh, her. Well yes and no. It kind of backfired because I think she was upset with me for paying attention to Lexi and not to her."

Matt added, "When Sebastian was on that flight he had just caught his girlfriend, you know, the actress Amanda Evans, with another man. Anyway, he got drunk, which is understandable under the circumstances. He can't be held accountable for his behavior because he was going through a very difficult time personally."

"I see. Getting back to Ms. Parker. Would you say that she was very jealous of Miss Lincoln?" Agent Young persisted.

"Yeah, I guess so. But I'm not sure if she was jealous of Lexi or just upset with me for not flirting back with her. I think that's why she and Greg went on that talk show to bash me. How did this become about me?" Sebastian asked.

Sebastian didn't like the way things were progressing. The Leech had Lexi, clearly. If the FBI would just get The Leech, then they could find out if anyone else was working with him. But from what Sebastian had heard from Jennifer at Rolling Pines, The Leech didn't need any help. He was crazy enough to pull things off on his own.

"Mr. Hawk. I am only trying to gather facts."

"Yes, you said that, Agent Young, but you have been somewhat accusatory of Sebastian here," Matt interrupted. He was getting annoyed. "All he wants to do is help you guys find Lexi. He had nothing to do with her disappearance! Do we need to call a lawyer?"

"Matt, relax. Agent Young is just doing his job. He's very thorough and I appreciate that," Sebastian said trying to neutralize the situation, even though he too was upset with Agent Young.

"Thank you, Mr. Hawk. As for the property that you found on the computer, I did some research and discovered that it is no longer owned by Mr. Orrington. The sale went through last month but it hasn't appeared in public records yet."

"Really? The guy did real estate transactions while in a mental hospital? How is that possible?" Sebastian was surprised.

"Perhaps someone has his power of attorney," Agent Young suggested.

Sebastian nodded his head. "I guess that could happen. So does this mean that we're back to square one?"

"No, quite to the contrary. You've provided me with quite a bit of useful information and we have a lot of resources at our disposal here at the FBI. I'm sure we will zero in on Miss Lincoln's whereabouts soon," Agent Young said confidently. "We'll get her." He stood up and held out his hand. Evidently the meeting was over.

They shook his hand. "Please keep me updated. I'm going crazy worrying about her," Sebastian told him.

"I will. And let me know if you get any more phone calls or messages so I can listen to the communications."

When Matt and Sebastian left, Sebastian was feeling more confused than ever. Was it The Leech who had Lexi or could it possibly be someone else who took her? It had to be The Leech, he decided. He was the one making the threats. He was the logical choice.

Chapter 19 – Discoveries

"Mr. Hawk," Margarit called to Sebastian as soon as he walked through the garage door.

"What, Margarit?"

"I have something I want to show you."

Sebastian and Matt followed Margarit up to Sebastian's bedroom.

"I found this in your bathroom closet. I don't think I ever saw it before and the bathroom is a strange place for it, so I thought I'd better tell you right away."

"Thank you," he replied as she handed it to him. Margarit left the room.

"Whose is that?" Matt asked.

"It's Lexi's. I guess it fell out of her bag."

Sebastian brought it downstairs to his office. "I wonder what's on here," he said curiously.

Sebastian was sure finding Lexi's laptop computer would hold the key to the whole thing.

He couldn't wait to go through it.

Matt stayed at Sebastian's house longer than he intended, even though he had other things he needed to be doing. He couldn't drag himself away from all the drama. He was too invested. Too engrossed. Too nosy.

Sebastian was eager to look through Lexi's e-mails. But he needed her password to access them. Damn! *What could it be?* he wondered. He tried everything he knew to be associated with her. Teeth? Denied. Dentist? Nope. Atlanta? Wrong password. Greg? Please try again.

"Shit! What's her birthday? Maybe that's it," Sebastian said aloud.

"No, not her birthday," Matt told him. "Women don't do that stuff. They like personal things. Try something not everyone would know about her," Matt suggested.

Suddenly Matt was an expert on women?

"How am I supposed to know what that is? I just met her!" Sebastian was frustrated. "Wait!" He typed his needle in the haystack idea – 'Mary' – and with a huge stroke of luck, they were in!

"You're good!" Matt said.

"Call me Bond. James Bond," Sebastian gloated.

"So what are we looking for exactly?" Matt asked.

"I'm not sure. Let me hit the *find* key and see if there is anything for 'leech'."

Nothing came up. Then Sebastian typed in

'Travis' and he found an e-mail from Lexi to her mother from last year.

"No, Mom, I haven't heard anything about Travis in a long time, thank goodness. I think he's out of my life for good. Finally!" he read aloud.

That was useless. *Think Sebastian, think*, he told himself. He had no idea what to do so he just started reading her mail. He began at the top with the unopened mail. There were several letters talking about him. Apparently her friends had all seen the footage and thought Sebastian was gorgeous. While that boosted his ego, it didn't help move things forward. Then he saw a new letter from Greg.

Lexi, I can't believe what happened in California. I'm still in shock about the whole thing. I had a long flight home and really thought about everything, about us. There was this nice flight attendant who chatted with me. Even though I am still appalled by your public display of affection with a total stranger, like I told you in LA, I forgive you for that because I get the whole celebrity appeal. Unfortunately, James turned out to be such a loser. But that's neither here nor there. I still shouldn't have hit him. I have no excuse for my behavior. If I reacted that way it's only because I must really care about you. I've decided to give you another chance. Please call me as soon as you get this and I'll meet you at the airport in Atlanta so we can begin making up! Greg.

Sebastian wanted to gag when he read the

letter. *Ugh!* At first he thought this guy had no balls. Then Sebastian realized that he must have sounded the same way to Amanda, which meant that he was actually every bit the loser he had accused Greg of being. That sucked. It was hard to see himself from an outside perspective, and from that vantage point, the view was not pretty.

"Well, I don't think Greg is working with The Leech, not that I ever did. But this confirms it, don't you agree?"

Matt read the letter. "Yeah. I think this leech guy is on his own. He's just a nut."

Sebastian's phone rang. This time he looked to see what it said. 'Private number.' He answered it on speakerphone so Matt could hear, in case it was The Leech.

"Hello?"

"Stay away from Mary. She's mine."

Sebastian quickly responded, before The Leech had time to hang up.

"But she's with you. You have her, right?"

There was a long silence. Sebastian didn't hear any hang up so he spoke again, "Where do you have Mary, Travis? What did you do with her?"

The Leech replied. "You kissed Mary."

"Yes, but she's with you now, right?"

"I want Mary. Give me Mary," he said with his voice getting elevated.

"I don't have Mary. You have Mary," Sebastian insisted.

More silence.

"Where are you, Travis?"

Dial tone.

Sebastian's heart was racing. So was Matt's. After taking a split second to digest what had just happened, Sebastian called Agent Young.

"I'm glad you called," Agent Young told him. "I'll pull up the call and listen right away to see if there's anything we can get from it."

"Great!" Sebastian said excitedly.

"I have some more news for you, Mr. Hawk," Agent Young told him.

"What?"

"We believe we have located Mr. Orrington and several of our agents will be making a raid on his home after dark tonight. Miss Lincoln should be recovered at that time."

"WHAT? REALLY? Tonight? That's fantastic! Where?"

"I can't tell you that, but I will call you when it's all over," Agent Young promised.

Sebastian turned to Matt and repeated the news. Then he said to Agent Young, "Oh, by the way, I found Lexi's computer. It was at my house. But I guess you don't need it now, do you?"

"Actually, I would still like to keep it for evidence. Can you please bring it to my office?"

"For evidence? There's nothing really useful on it, though. I've been looking through her mail and found nothing earth-shattering."

"Mr. Hawk. You had no right to look through Miss Lincoln's computer. That is considered evidence in a federal crime investigation. I insist that you turn it over to me immediately."

"Okay, man, calm down. I had no idea I did anything wrong. I was just trying to help. Sorry. I'll bring it over now."

"Thank you. Goodbye."

"Bye."

Matt decided to stay at Sebastian's house to do some work while Sebastian drove the computer to the FBI building. Maybe if Matt had joined Sebastian he would have noticed the small silver car that followed behind. It wasn't until Sebastian was in the government building's parking lot, and the silver car pulled up right next to him, that he knew he was tailed.

"What's going on Sebastian? Are you in some kind of trouble? This is a government building, right? Do you have jury duty? Give us something," the reporter prodded as his photographer snapped photos of Sebastian.

"Hi, guys. Just going to do some research for my role. It's always good to hone my skills during the off-season," he lied.

"What's your relationship like with Amanda Evans now?"

"We're still good friends." He lied again.

"What about that Lexi Lincoln woman? Are you two dating?"

"Sorry guys, but I have an appointment

here and I'm running a little late. Have a good afternoon," he said as he walked into the building.

Sebastian handed the laptop to Agent Young and told him how pleased he was that the FBI was able to find Travis and Lexi so quickly. Sebastian was dying to go with them for the raid, but he knew there was no way Agent Young, or anyone at the FBI for that matter, would allow him to tag along, so he didn't bother to ask.

When Sebastian left Agent Young's office he exhaled for the first time in a couple of days. He was so relieved that it would all be over soon. He really did have to get back to his own life and start thinking about how to salvage whatever was left of his fan base.

Sebastian decided to celebrate, albeit prematurely, by going to a restaurant for a hot meal. This was normal for him, dining alone. He liked the solitude and he also liked to people watch. As much as he was an actor, he was also a fan, and sometimes he would run into fellow actors or actresses whom he admired.

Sebastian sat down at a table and was just served a cup of coffee when his phone rang. His blood pressure shot right up when he saw those dreaded words, 'private number.'

"Hi Mr. Hawk. This is Lisa Wells from *24-Hour Hollywood*. We were wondering if you'd like to be interviewed today for our show. You must have some opinions about everything that's gone on this week," she said.

Sebastian breathed a sigh of relief that it wasn't The Leech, but at the same time it wasn't a welcome call either, at least not right then.

"I'm sorry, Lisa, but my calendar today is full. I'll check with my manager and publicist to see when I can work it in. I'd like to talk with you, really, I would. Hopefully sometime very soon. Thanks for the offer."

"But Mr. Hawk, –"

"Hang on, Lisa, my phone's beeping – Hello?"

"How much is Mary worth to you?" the voice asked.

"Is she okay? I need to know she's okay," Sebastian responded.

"Yes."

"Send me a picture of her." Finally, something Detective James Gilbert would say.

The caller disappeared so Sebastian hung up, but the phone rang again because he was still connected to Lisa.

"Sorry, Lisa, but I've got to run. I'll be in touch," Sebastian said as he hung up on her.

He called Agent Young immediately to tell him of the call and then he ordered his food. All of the stress had taken a toll on Sebastian and his appetite had been smaller than usual the last few days, but when his food arrived, he surprised himself by digging right in. It was delicious and he ate until he was so full he almost felt sick. Just as he was about to pay the bill, his phone went off. He had a text message – picture mail.

Sebastian held his breath as he opened it. Yes, it was a picture of Lexi! She was cute as could be. She was wearing a dark green t-shirt and, though she looked raggedy, she appeared unharmed. Sebastian was thrilled. He quickly forwarded the photo to Agent Young and then threw money onto the table and drove home. In only a few hours, he would have Lexi back in his arms.

Chapter 20 – The Raid Date

Lexi read the *Cosmopolitan* magazine that he brought her. It was the latest issue, which meant he must have gone out to pick one up especially for her, after she requested something to read to help her pass her time in captivity.

"Excuse me," she said while knocking on the inside of her door. "Are you out there?"

"What is it now?" he asked. She could hear him approaching the room.

"Do you think I could freshen up? I still have all my make-up on from the banquet two nights ago. It's not good to keep that stuff on my skin too long. See, it says in the article right here that people can get all kinds of bacteria in their skin if they don't take their make-up off in a timely manner." She spoke through the door but still held up the magazine article as though she was showing it to him.

He unlocked the door and looked at Lexi. She was a pretty mess and he was very attracted to her. He wanted her to be happy, if at all possible under the circumstances. But he also wanted to make himself happy, which was the point of the whole abduction...his happiness.

"Here's the thing. I'll give you a choice," he told Lexi. "You can stay the way you are, dirty, or you can take a shower...with me in the bathroom watching."

"What? You want to watch me shower?" Lexi became scared. She felt so vulnerable. "I'll stay dirty, thanks anyway."

"Suit yourself." He walked out and locked the door. She sat on her mattress and continued to read the magazine. She knew she had to come up with an escape plan and she hoped maybe there would be something in the magazine that would spark a good idea.

"Oh good, you're back," Matt said when Sebastian returned to his home office. "The Leech responded to your Internet post – 'Mary is never going to be yours.' Look, he wrote back, 'Mary will be mine. You're a liar youdontknowjack28.'"

Sebastian looked at it, but he wasn't very concerned with anything that The Leech was posting. It would all come to an end soon, only The Leech didn't know it.

Sebastian told Matt about his outing – from

the reporters who followed him, to the picture of Lexi, to Lisa Wells from *24-Hour Hollywood*. Matt was interested in all of it, especially the call from Lisa Wells. He couldn't help himself. He was just programmed that way. Matt was all publicity, all the time.

Matt contacted Wayne about *24-Hour Hollywood*'s offer. They discussed Sebastian's precarious situation and his fairly open schedule. Sebastian didn't have any work projects coming up in the near future so, as far as Wayne was concerned, he could go on *24-Hour Hollywood* whenever he felt like it. But Wayne tried to impress upon Matt that he let Sebastian finish with the Lexi thing and give him a moment to regroup before throwing Sebastian to the press wolves. It would only hurt Sebastian and his career if he wasn't emotionally up to the task, Wayne explained. Matt reluctantly agreed.

Sebastian's phone rang. The caller ID said 'LAPD'. He answered the call. "Hello?"

"Hello, Sebastian. This is Detective Miller, you know, Gwen."

"Oh, yes. Hi, Gwen."

"Hi. I've been in touch with Agent Young and he told me that they've made great progress, thanks in part to your help." She flattered Sebastian's male ego and he ate it right up.

"Well, you know, even though I only portray a detective, I've still learned quite a bit. Every week I'm solving crimes, much like you!" he said lightheartedly.

"Yes, I suppose that's true. Anyway, I was thinking about how worried you've been about Ms. Lincoln and I was wondering if you wanted to go with me to witness the raid on Mr. Orrington later?"

That was the most exciting offer a woman had made to him in years.

"ABSOLUTELY!" Sebastian enthusiastically replied.

"I believe it's quite a drive so I'll pick you up at around six-ish tonight. It might take us a few hours to get there."

"Where is it?" he asked.

"I can't tell you that. You're just going to have to trust me," she said flirtatiously.

"Alright. I'm in your hands! Did you say you want to come here to get me?"

"Yes. I'll come to you. But I can only bring you, not Sam. I'm bending the rules a bit as it is," she explained.

"Fine. Just me. I can't wait. Thank you so much, Gwen. I'll see you later."

"Yes you will, bye," Gwen said as she hung up.

"What was that all about? You look like a kid who just got his first woody," Matt eloquently asked.

"Shut up, Matt. It was Gwen, you know, Detective Miller. She invited me to go with her to tonight's raid! I think we might be on a date, actually, but who cares? I'm going to be there when they rescue Lexi and witness them locking up that son of a bitch Travis!"

"You're going on a raid date? That's a new one!" Matt teased.

They both laughed. "Yeah, it's crazy, I know."

Matt told Sebastian that as much as he wanted to hang out there, he had other matters he had to attend to, so he left.

Sebastian went upstairs to his room. He thought it would be a good idea to take a brief power nap so he would be energized for the big night. He was quite excited about the upcoming events and he knew that if he didn't try to sleep, he would just spend the rest of the afternoon pacing and watching the clock. He figured this was just like going to bed so Santa would come sooner. All Sebastian wanted from Santa was an unharmed Lexi. He'd never wished harder for a present.

Sebastian had trouble falling asleep because there were so many thoughts spinning around in his head. But he made himself lie in bed for a couple of hours until it was time for him to get up and get prepared for the night.

After he was nearly ready, he checked his cell phone and saw he had missed a text. He hoped it was from Lexi. It wasn't. Just Sam checking in. He wrote back to Sam to let him know the good news – that he was going to help the FBI rescue Lexi. Sam wrote back that he was happy and relieved.

Since Sebastian knew Gwen had a little crush on him, and because he felt indebted to her for bringing him along on the raid, he thought it would be appropriate to order dinner for them. As a very chivalrous guy, Sebastian was in the habit of buying women meals, which just added to his natural charisma. But ordering food deliveries was usually his assistant's forte. Since the S.O.B. was no longer in Sebastian's life, he searched the Internet for the phone number of his favorite Chinese restaurant. He called and ordered a large assortment of dishes. After all, he didn't know what Gwen liked. Plus, Sebastian thought that once they got Lexi, she would be hungry too, so it would be good to have a little extra food.

The delivery guy came and went, and then Gwen arrived. He invited her in, but she suggested they get right on the road. She really wanted to go inside, but she heard on the radio about traffic issues in the direction they were heading, so she would have to wait for another opportunity to be alone with Sebastian in his home. In the meantime, she was quite delighted to have him in her car. Just being around Sebastian made her feel giddy.

"What's all this?" Gwen asked as Sebastian got into the car with three large paper bags.

"Dinner! I thought we could have a picnic. You must be hungry." He was very gallant.

"Wow, there's a lot of stuff there. What did you get?" Gwen loved that Sebastian knew she wanted to be treated like any other woman, not just a detective. It made her like him even more.

As Gwen drove, Sebastian spouted off the menu for the evening. It was a good thing he had such an excellent memory because he was able to recall the comprehensive list of items he ordered. Gwen laughed to herself about the excessive amount of food he brought, but she didn't say a word to Sebastian. It was sweet of him to even think about bringing dinner along.

"Sebastian, tell me about yourself."

"There's not much to tell," he responded. "I'm a Midwesterner who got bit by the acting bug. But what I want to know is how did a beautiful woman like you decide to become a detective?" He could be quite a charmer when he wanted to be.

"My dad's a cop and my mother's a stunt woman. I guess I was genetically engineered for it," she said.

"A stunt woman? Really? That must be how you became the strong, fearless woman you are." Sebastian was laying it on thick and he knew it. But he was so happy to be included in Lexi's rescue that paying Gwen compliments seemed to be a good way for him to express his thanks.

"Yeah, Mom still does it, but not as often as she used to. She's a grandmother now so she doesn't heal as quickly these days."

"You have kids?"

"No, but my sister has a four-year-old son and a two-year-old daughter. They're beyond adorable and so smart!" Gwen lit up when she spoke about them.

"I bet. It must be such fun to have a niece and nephew. Do they live nearby? Do you get to play with them a lot?" he wanted to know.

"Yeah, they're not far from me at all. On my days off I take them to the park and we all go down the slide. We have little songs we sing in the car. They're a blast."

"It sounds like it. I love kids. They're so pure and open. As an actor, you can never fool a kid. They're like dogs, you know. They have great instincts!" Sebastian chuckled.

"Yeah, and they don't wet the rug like dogs, well, not anymore!" Gwen laughed.

"Do you have any pets?" he asked her.

The small talk went on for the two and a half hour drive. It was a nice change for Sebastian who had spent the last week discussing his and Lexi's personal miseries. It was good to have some time away from the heartbreaking reality of their lives.

Gwen enjoyed her time with Sebastian, too. He was even more wonderful than she had imagined. It troubled her a bit though, when she thought about the fact that they were on their way to rescue his newest girlfriend. Would Gwen be yesterday's news once he reunited with Lexi? Gwen decided she didn't care. She would simply enjoy their time together.

Gwen pulled her car into a shopping center's lot and parked.

"They're *here*?" Sebastian asked.

"No. This is where we wait and meet up with

the others. That car over there is with us," she said while pointing to a tan Ford.

She continued, "Let's dig into that food. I'm sure it's cold by now, but it smells great."

"Chinese food is best when it's cold," Sebastian told her.

"True."

They ate right out of the boxes. Unfortunately, some of the sauce had leaked out of the bag, spilling onto the backseat of her car. Sebastian felt terrible about it but Gwen was pretty cool.

"Don't worry about it, really. I'll bill it to the taxpayers," she joked.

Sebastian wanted to laugh, but as the time got closer to Lexi's big rescue, his nerves mounted. When would the others get there? How much longer would they have to wait? One by one cars arrived. Some were plain, nondescript. Others had lights on their roofs or dashboards.

They were pretty much done eating, though the two of them barely put a dent into the buffet Sebastian had provided, when Gwen's phone rang.

"Yeah...Okay...We will. Got it." She hung up.

"What was that about? What did they say?" Sebastian asked anxiously.

"That was Agent Young. He said I should follow Agent Morris in the white car to the block where the house is and then wait on the corner."

"Wait on the corner? Will we be able to see what's happening from there?"

"Don't know. We're only here to observe. We

can't get in their way," Gwen explained.

"Oh." Sebastian was disappointed. The testosterone in him wanted to be in the action. But he knew Matt would be very happy that they were not.

All of the government cars quickly dispersed and Gwen followed the white car down a few roads until she stopped at a corner.

"We're here. It's that house over there." Gwen pointed to a yellow house half way down the street. There was a lamppost on the sidewalk immediately in front of its front door which gave Sebastian a clear view, even though it was night. His heart was racing with anticipation.

Chapter 21 – Finding The Leech

A swarm of agents surrounded the small yellow house. It looked like bees circling a hive. Then suddenly, it happened.

Sebastian couldn't hear what was going on from where he and Gwen were situated so she gave him a play-by-play of what they were likely to be saying.

"First, they'll knock loudly on the front door and shout, 'OPEN UP! FBI!' Usually around that time, the people inside are scrambling, looking for hiding places or weapons," Gwen explained.

But that didn't happen. Sebastian watched as the door opened. The agents showed their badges and their search warrant to the man standing in front of them, presumably Travis Orrington, and then they all walked inside.

"What's happening? Why didn't they throw him to the ground and put handcuffs on him? That's what would have happened on *Crime Days and Nights*," Sebastian said to Gwen.

"It's not over yet, Sebastian. Let's wait to see what happens," she tried to assure him.

Outside of the house the other agents were still on high alert with their weapons drawn, prepared for any scenario that might develop. It was exhilarating to watch and both Gwen and Sebastian's hearts were tense. Sebastian impatiently observed as several more agents entered the house.

"What's taking so long?" he muttered.

After twenty minutes it was over, peacefully. The agents walked out of the house, got back into their cars and left the scene, but they had no one in their custody.

"What happened?" Sebastian insisted. "Where's Lexi?"

"I don't know. We've been instructed to reconvene in the parking lot for a briefing," Gwen told him.

Everyone drove back to the shopping center, except this time the agents got out of their cars for a meeting. Sebastian was asked to wait in Gwen's car but there was no way that was going to happen. He got out and stood with the others.

Sebastian couldn't believe what they said. Lexi wasn't there? Travis wasn't breaking any laws? This was a bad lead? How was that possible?

The agents took it in stride and left after their meeting. Sebastian got back into Gwen's car feeling very angry and also a bit hopeless.

"I don't understand," he said to her. "How can they say it's a bad lead? This guy took Lexi! Why didn't they look harder to find her? Maybe he has her hidden somewhere in the yard, like inside a shed or in a hole in the ground? Or maybe he's keeping her captive someplace else, off the premises. Didn't they ever consider that?" he asked desperately. "This is insane! Detective James Gilbert never would have quit so quickly." Sebastian was outraged.

Gwen responded in a calming tone. "Sebastian, I know you must be extremely upset right now, but if Agent Young said Mr. Orrington is not the kidnapper, then he must be right. He has been doing this for many years and he knows what to look for. I don't think Mr. Orrington could have outsmarted Agent Young."

"I know The Leech isn't brilliant, I'm not saying he is, but it's entirely possible that he has Lexi somewhere else, don't you think? Maybe he has someone helping him. I want to speak with Agent Young. I'm going to call him."

"You can call him if that helps you feel better," Gwen said.

"What would help me feel better is if Lexi was safely back with me," he said in an irritated tone. "Sorry, I don't mean to take this out on you. But I'm really mad!"

"Agent Young," he answered his phone.

"This is Sebastian Hawk. What the hell just

happened? Where's Lexi?"

"Mr. Hawk, we did a thorough search of Mr. Orrington's property and there was no evidence whatsoever that he was holding Miss Lincoln."

"But we know he's been stalking her," Sebastian pointed out. "And then suddenly he calls us and says that she belongs to him? And then she disappears? Come on! How can you tell me he has nothing to do with this? That's ridiculous!"

"Mr. Hawk, I agree that there was a lot of circumstantial evidence indicating his involvement in Miss Lincoln's disappearance, which is what prompted the raid. However, after interviewing Mr. Orrington, I am no longer convinced that he had anything to do with it. As for making phone calls and posting things on the Internet, that is not illegal. Yes, we found pictures of Miss Lincoln in his house, but again, Mr. Orrington's obsession does not necessarily mean that he's a kidnapper."

"What about the ransom request he made?" Sebastian asked.

"We don't know that was him necessarily, do we? It may have been a copycat."

"A copycat?"

"Yes, someone who was aware of his threats and used that information to their advantage by framing Mr. Orrington for their crime. I believe that's what's going on here," Agent Young said with certainty.

"Who would do something like that? And why would anyone want to kidnap Lexi?" Sebastian asked.

"That's what I'm going to figure out."

"Agent Young. We're all headed back to LA. I'd like to ride back with you so we can discuss this further. Maybe I can be of some help to you in solving this. You know I play a detective on TV."

"Mr. Hawk. I understand your disappointment, but this is real life, not a television show. Please let us do our jobs. You have already given me quite a bit of information that I will review again tomorrow when I get back to my office. I suggest in the meantime you try to put your mind onto other things. We WILL find her."

"Yeah. Fine." Sebastian hung up angrily.

Gwen listened to the conversation and knew there was no point in continuing to flirt with Sebastian the rest of the night. He was in a bad mood and would likely remain that way, which she understood. They drove back without conversation. Just the radio played. It was a long couple of hours.

"Sam," Sebastian spoke into his phone when he was back home.

"Hello, sir. How did it go? Is Miss Lexi safe?" he asked with hope in his voice.

"No. She wasn't there."

"Was it the wrong place?" he asked.

"No, they found The Leech, only he didn't have Lexi. That must be why he keeps telling me that he wants her. He really doesn't have her. Can you believe that?" Sebastian said, exasperated.

"I don't understand. So where's Lexi then?"

"They don't know. They think a copycat criminal kidnapped her. Someone who knew about the whole leech situation and tried to pin it on him," Sebastian explained. "This whole thing gets crazier and crazier by the minute."

"I'm sorry, Sebastian. Do you want me to come over?" Sam offered.

"No. I'm going to try to get some sleep tonight and then – hang on, my phone's beeping, maybe it's Lexi – Hello?" Sebastian answered.

"How much is Mary worth to you?"

"How much do you want for her?" Sebastian countered.

"Five million dollars," he said emphatically.

Sebastian was shocked but didn't want to show it so he said, "Fine. It's yours. Where is she."

"You'll get her when I get my money."

"I want another picture. How do I know she's still okay?" Sebastian demanded.

"No. No more pictures."

"Then let me speak to her or no money," Sebastian said firmly. He knew he was pressing his luck, but he had to hear her voice.

"Sebastian, it's me. I miss you. I'm –"

"Okay? She's fine. I'll call you tomorrow with instructions on how we can make the exchange."

"I don't know how long it will take for me to get that kind of money. It's not like I have it in my wallet."

"Go to your bank. Sell your stocks and bonds. You can get it. We'll talk tomorrow." And he hung up.

"Sam, are you still there?" Sebastian asked as he clicked back to their call.

"Yes."

"It was the kidnapper. Sorry to hang up on you, but I've gotta call Agent Young. Bye."

Lexi was in her room when he walked in with the phone. He called Sebastian and then shoved the phone in her face. "Say you're okay," she was told. He was using a disguised voice on the call. Lexi found that interesting. Kidnapping 101, she assumed. Lexi wished she'd been able to give Sebastian some kind of clue as to where she was, but she didn't actually know where she was and besides, there was no time for her to think. It all happened so fast.

Lexi heard her captor ask for a ridiculous amount of money. Sebastian doesn't have that much, she assumed. How could he ever come up with a ransom like that? But she decided not to worry about it. Sebastian was smart and he must know lots of rich people who maybe would help him get his hands of that kind of cash.

Being held for a ransom comforted Lexi. She figured it meant she wouldn't be chopped up and scattered in the woods because he needed something to sell – her. Lexi felt a bit of power shift her way. She became less afraid.

"I've decided that I want to wash up. If you have to be a pervert about the whole thing and watch me, then you do what you have to do," she said bravely.

Her kidnapper was so happy that he would soon be getting his money that seeing Lexi naked was simply the icing on his creepy cake.

"Great!" he said. "Let's go."

"Are you going to watch me pee, too? Can't I at least do that in private?"

"Fine. Pee. Then I'm coming in."

"Lexi ran the faucet while she peed and tried to type a quick text into her phone, but the phone's battery was already dead. She put the phone back into the cabinet and flushed the toilet.

Showering in front of someone was strange, but Lexi tried not to think about his beady eyes watching her. She sang a song in her head and imagined she was back in Atlanta in her own bathroom. She showered her fastest shower in history and, amazingly, he was true to his word and only watched from the other side of the shower door. When she stepped out, he wrapped her in a white towel and then copped a feel. As she felt him squeeze her breasts, she prayed he wouldn't touch her anywhere else. It was a miracle, but he didn't.

Fortunately for Lexi, he wasn't a rapist. He'd decided right before he took her that he wouldn't force himself on Lexi in that way. He was merely a business man doing a financial transaction.

After she dried off, he handed Lexi different clothes to put on. Prettier clothes. A creme colored sundress with black flip flops. She asked him to bring her the plastic goody bag she was given at the banquet and explained that there was a toothbrush and toothpaste in it. He found the bag, tossed it to her, and walked away as she brushed her teeth. He was in the other room when she took something else out of the bag and hid it in her underwear.

Even though it was quite late at night, Lexi asked to stay out of her room for a bit and watch TV, as a reward for being so cooperative. He was enamored with Lexi, especially after his personal peep show. He thought she was sexy and also quite brave.

"Come sit with me. That's fine," he told her.

She sat on the other end of the faded blue sofa that was in the small living room in the apartment. There was a brown, wooden coffee table in front of them that he put his feet on. She looked over at him, in between watching TV. He looked like such a normal person. What would drive someone to act that way?

Lexi made small talk in hopes of developing his trust. They discussed the weather. Los Angeles. And TV shows. When she asked him about *Crime Days and Nights,* he became upset.

"It's a piece of shit show with piece of shit actors. It's insane that it's been on so long. There's absolutely no reason why that show should be a success!" he said angrily.

Wow. She had hit a nerve. She wasn't much of a crime show fan either, but she thought a kidnapper would have found that stuff enjoyable or at least maybe educational.

Lexi didn't know what to think about him. But she was relieved that she was clean and would likely live to see another day – and hopefully, the rest of her natural life.

Chapter 22 – Big Break

Sebastian was at Agent Young's office before Agent Young. He sat impatiently on a bench by the elevator awaiting his arrival. Finally, Agent Young showed up and they went into his office to discuss the situation.

While Agent Young appreciated the help that Sebastian offered, he wasn't very happy about Sebastian's intense involvement in the case. He liked to work alone, but he knew he had no choice here. Sebastian wasn't going away until Lexi was found.

"The kidnapper's been in touch with you again. I listened to the call. He wants five million dollars." Agent Young confirmed.

"Yes, that's what he said. What should I do?" Sebastian asked.

"Sebastian, I was wondering about these phone calls. You said you had some from Mr. Orrington and now we realize that some were from the real kidnapper who pretended to be Mr. Orrington as well. Why didn't you notice a difference in their voices?"

"I know I should've, and I'm usually really good about that stuff, but I just got kind of thrown off each time the calls came in. I was never really prepared. And, you know, I thought it was always The Leech, so I guess I didn't pay attention to any differences in the voices. I'm sorry."

"Just listen closely the next time you receive a call to determine if there is anything recognizable about the voice."

"Okay, I will," Sebastian responded. "But what am I supposed to do about the money?"

"He told you to sell your stocks and bonds."

"Yeah. Should I sell my investments?" Sebastian asked.

"Do you have that much money in stocks and bonds, Mr. Hawk?"

"I think so, just about, altogether."

"I don't think it will be necessary for you to gather the money. You just have to make him think you're moving forward. Try to stall him without upsetting him, while we zero in on their whereabouts. And keep calling him The Leech, like you've done. Don't let him know that we've discovered his secret."

"Okay. I'll string him along while you solve the puzzle. Please let me know if I can be of any further assistance."

They shook hands goodbye.

Sebastian had read stories about people who were desperate for their fifteen minutes of fame and would risk anything to have it. *What a great way to get well-known*, he thought. *Kidnap someone connected to a celebrity. If they get away with it, they get millions of dollars. If they get caught, the whole world will know their name. It's a win-win situation for nutjobs.*

Sebastian thought about all of the crackpots who watched him and Lexi on TV or saw them on the Internet. Any one of them could be the kidnapper. By taking Lexi, some maniac could get a big payday and at the same time put Sebastian in the poorhouse. All it would take was one crazy opportunist looking to cash in.

As Sebastian drove home, his mind was racing in a million directions. Just as he pulled his car into his garage, his phone rang. 'Private number.' He knew who it was this time. He just knew.

"Hello," Sebastian said.

"Do you have the money?"

"Listen, Leech, it takes a long time to do all that stuff. I called my broker and he's putting in sell bids, but because the market's been down lately he doesn't think I can raise that much money right now."

There was silence on the phone.

Sebastian continued, "I don't know what else to tell you. I have nothing in the bank because I just spent a ton of money on a vacation to St. Thomas that I didn't get to take. That money went down the drain. And now a lot more of it's going to be lost by selling in this depressed market."

"How much can you get?" the voice asked.

"I'll have to let you know tomorrow," Sebastian stalled.

"I'll call you at the end of today. Figure something out. I want all five million."

The caller hung up and Sebastian called Agent Young to tell him to play back the recorded call.

Agent Young called Sebastian after he listened to the conversation. "You did great!" Agent Young said with surprising animation. He was such a dry guy that a compliment from him felt especially good to Sebastian.

"What should I tell him at the end of today?"

"Keep stalling. I'm working on this all day. Maybe we'll have some solid leads by then."

"Really? You think you can make progress that fast?" Sebastian asked.

"I was just reading in my notes that when Lexi texted you, she indicated she was not too far away. That gives us a parameter to work in. I'm going to follow some hunches and see who turns up nearby."

"That's great! I'll let you know when I speak with him later, Agent Young."

"Good."

They both hung up.

Sebastian wondered how it was possible that The Leech wasn't involved in this at all. Then he considered that maybe one of Lexi's father's criminal friends was behind it. There were just so many variables to consider it was overwhelming. Fortunately Sebastian had faith in Agent Young and decided to give him time to do his job. He needed to believe that this guy knew his business. He needed to hold on to hope.

Sebastian went into his house and called Matt. For the first time in a while, Sebastian was ready to discuss his career. Getting back to his own reality helped pass the time. It was also important that Sebastian take an active role in damage control. Perhaps it was the right time for him to go on *24-Hour Hollywood* and confront the rumors. Perhaps it wasn't the right time to do that, while he was in the middle of an FBI investigation. He and Matt needed to figure out what his next move should be.

Lexi slept long and hard for the first time in several days. The mattress was comfortable enough, and since he hadn't hit her or hurt her yet, she had no reason to think that he would surprise her with a middle of the night attack. She also took comfort in knowing she had devised a plan. She would put it into motion as soon as the opportunity presented itself.

When the morning came, she could hear him on the phone and then on the computer. She knocked on her door.

"Now what?" he complained.

"I need to go to the bathroom!"

"Alright," he responded.

He opened the door and she used the bathroom. When Lexi came out of the bathroom, she smiled her powerful smile at him. He wanted to be tough, but, like most men, he was softened by her broad grin.

"You have a beautiful smile," he told her.

"Thank you. You know that's what I do for a living, right? Help people have shiny teeth. You would be super handsome if your teeth were just a little bit brighter," she said, trying not to sound insulting.

"I don't care about shiny teeth," he grumbled. "Get back in your room."

Was now the right time to put her plan into effect? His guard was down and she was out of her room. Action!

"You have an eyelash poking into your eye," she said sweetly. "Don't you feel it? Doesn't it bother you?"

He took his hand and tried to twist his lashes upward.

"Oh, you actually made it worse. Do you want me to get it for you? Sit down over here," she said while pointing to the sofa.

"It's fine."

"Are you sure? Because those things can be a real nuisance. They make your eyes tear nonstop. It could cause an infection. Come on. Let me help you."

He looked at Lexi in her dress. She was
so small and feminine. So nonthreatening. He
complied. He sat on the sofa and said, "Fine, pull it
out."

Lexi told him to close his eyes for just a
second, which he did. She pulled the tube of teeth
whitening gel out of her underwear, squeezed some
onto her fingertips and rubbed the toxic goo all
over his eyes.

"AHHHHHHHHHHHH! SHIIIIITTTTTTTTTT!" he
hollered.

While he was blinded from the acidic
ingredients, she ran out the front door of the
apartment screaming "Heeeeeelp!" and knocked on
several of the apartment doors in the hallway. No
one opened up. Lexi spotted the exit stairwell and
then ran down the steps as fast as she could to get
herself outside to freedom. He tried to run after her
but the pain was excruciating and he couldn't see
a thing. Lexi frantically sprinted down the street,
turned the corner and saw a bus. She waved it
down and got on.

"Go, please go!" she said with panic in her
voice. The bus moved along, but Lexi didn't have
any money.

"Are you going to pay?" the driver asked her.

"I need to get to a police station. Is there one
nearby? I just escaped from being kidnapped," she
said. She was panting and tears began exploding
out of her eyes. She wiped them as best she could,

careful not to put the teeth whitening gel into her own eyes. Water was running down her cheeks.

"Oh, my heavens!" an older woman with a short afro hairstyle and a Jamaican accent said. "Here, take this." She handed Lexi a napkin and also some money to give to the bus driver. "Come here, dear. Sit with me. You can use my phone."

Lexi was crying loudly when she called 911. With a cracking voice in between gasping for breaths she told the operator what had happened and gave him the number of the bus she was on. She was told that a police car would pick her up at the intersection of Long and 74th, which was two bus stops away. Lexi was very nervous to have to wait that long. Logically she knew there were other people around so she should be okay, but she was still afraid he would somehow catch up with her and snatch her back.

Everyone on the bus was watching the drama unfold, but Lexi was oblivious to their stares. Then, a man a few rows behind her spoke up, "Aren't you that girl I saw on TV? Yeah, you were the one kissing Sebastian Hawk."

Lexi didn't respond. When the bus came to its second stop she looked out the window, saw the police car and got off the bus. Finally, Lexi was safe.

When Sebastian was done talking with Matt he decided to get some exercise, which is why he didn't hear his phone ringing. He was on his elliptical machine and both his legs and his mind were racing. For a welcomed change, his thoughts weren't about Lexi, but about himself. Was Amanda right about all of the publicity being good for both of them? Should he speak with Wayne about trying to get a movie role? Maybe now was the time for him to make the big leap from television to feature films. What kind of movies could he get? Was he leading man material? He didn't want to play the best friend role, but then again, if it was a good part that paid well and moved his career forward, he should probably consider it.

Of course, the point was moot because no one had offered him any kind of movie role since he was twenty-one, when he turned down a small part in a slasher flick.

After a good long workout, Sebastian took a shower. He felt refreshed and relaxed. He walked out of his bedroom and could hear his cell phone ringing in the distance. Where had he put it? Then, as quickly as a flash of lightning, Sebastian's thoughts were transformed back into the stressful reality that was his current life. The kidnapper! He raced around his house looking for his phone. When he finally found it, the caller had already hung up.

Sebastian checked his missed calls log and saw he had two calls from the same number, a number he didn't recognize. Since he didn't know who they were from, he decided not to return the calls. He didn't need more surprises.

He carried his phone with him into his media room where he went to watch some sports. But his phone soon rang again. This time it was Agent Young's number that appeared in the caller ID.

"Hello," Sebastian answered.

"Mr. Hawk, I have some good news," he said.

Those were words that Sebastian was dying to hear.

"What?" he asked anxiously. "Do you know where they are?"

"Better. We HAVE Miss Lincoln. She's okay!"

"What? Really? Oh my God! Where is she? What happened?"

Sebastian's mind was spinning and so was his stomach. He never wanted to admit it, but he wasn't really buying the bullshit he kept telling himself about how everything would work out fine. He knew, deep down, that these things usually ended tragically.

"She's at the Pasadena police station," Agent Young informed him.

"Is she all right? Can I go see her? How did you catch him? Thank you, Agent Young. You're a true hero!"

"She's fine, but give her some time with the agents who are speaking with her. I'm headed over there now to join them," Agent Young said. Then he added, "You might want to know that Miss Lincoln is actually the hero. She escaped on her own."

"You're kidding! That woman is amazing!"

"Yes, she certainly seems to be. I'll call you when it's okay for you to come. All we have to do is find the dirtbag who did this to her and it will all be over."

"Thank you so much, Agent Young! Thank you!"

Sebastian called Sam, Matt, and Wayne to tell them the good news. He even considered calling Margarit but he wasn't sure how much she knew about the whole kidnapping thing and he didn't want to rehash it if she was unaware of all that went on.

The guys came over to Sebastian's house for an impromptu celebration. Sebastian ordered Thai food for everyone and asked Matt to pick up a couple of bottles of champagne. They ate and drank and laughed. It felt good for Sebastian to be relaxed and laughing. He hadn't done that in a while and it was beginning to seem like he would never feel happy again.

In the middle of their celebration Sebastian's phone rang. "It's Amanda," he said aloud.

"Don't answer it!" the guys instructed.

But, against his better judgment, he did.

"Hello," Sebastian said.

"Hi," Amanda replied.

Sebastian didn't say anything. He waited for her to speak again since she was the one who called him. He was in a great mood and he wasn't going to engage in a fight with her and ruin it.

"Um, Sebastian, I guess I just wanted to tell you how sorry I am about all that you've been going through this week. I know you told me about that stalker guy who was after your airplane girl, but I never knew that he actually kidnapped her. Oh, you poor baby. You must have been terrified. Thank goodness she's okay."

"How do you know about the kidnapping?" Sebastian was bewildered.

"It's on the news. There's video of her on a bus as she's escaping from that maniac. What a brave girl!"

"What channel?" he asked.

"All of them," Amanda replied.

"Guys, go turn on the TV, quick. The news!" Sebastian shouted. They all hurried into his media room and clicked on the TV.

"Thanks, Amanda. I really appreciate your concern. It's been rough. Thank God it's finally over."

"You can call me anytime you need to talk, you know that, don't you Sebastian?" she said nicely.

"I do now. Thanks. I've gotta go, though. Talk to you later."

"Okay, bye."

Sebastian and his entourage watched footage of Lexi on the bus calling the police. The video appeared to be taken with a cell phone.

The reporter said, "In just over a week's time, Sebastian Hawk has survived yet another nightmare. You may recall that he recently lost his girlfriend to another man, and now he almost lost a close friend to a killer. What an ordeal Mr. Hawk's been going through."

Matt was ecstatic! Finally, Sebastian was the victim. This would score huge sympathy points for him with women. He would be back on top for sure.

All Sebastian could think about, though, was Lexi. There she was, safe and sound. It was a wonderful image. One he would never forget.

Chapter 23 – Reconnecting

Lexi spent hours at the police station being interviewed by local police and the FBI. She told them everything she knew about her kidnapper but, because she wasn't from California, she couldn't provide them with the address of where she was being held. The bus route helped the authorities piece together her whereabouts.

Several police cars left in a caravan to capture the perpetrator. With Lexi waiting in a squad car nearby, the authorities burst into the apartment where she'd been kept. They found lots of evidence, but the kidnapper was gone. Lexi was escorted upstairs with two armed agents, one on either side of her. She was trembling as she entered the apartment. She showed them around the small place and then she was taken back to the police station.

Lexi's mind was everywhere. The whole

episode now seemed surreal to her. Was she really kidnapped? Had that actually happened? She asked if she could make some personal calls, so the officer handed her a phone and stepped away to give her some privacy.

"Mom, it's me."

"Oh, Mary! I just watched you on TV. I can't believe what you've been through. Are you okay?"

"Yeah, I guess so."

"Did he hurt you, honey?"

"No, I'm okay," Lexi replied.

"How could someone do this? It's a terrible world, you know."

"Yeah, Mom. Terrible. Did you say you saw me on TV?"Lexi asked.

"On the bus. It was on CNN," her mother told her.

"Someone filmed me on that bus?" Lexi couldn't believe the audacity of people. While she was running for her life, some jerk thought, *Hey this would make a good video?* How much more insane could the whole experience be?

"I love you, Mary," her mom said warmly.

"I love you too, Mom. I'd better go."

"Please come visit when you can, okay?"

"Yeah, I will. Send my love to everyone. Bye, Mom."

"Bye."

Lexi wanted to call Sebastian, but she didn't know his number by heart. It was programmed into her cell phone which had been placed into a baggie labeled "evidence". She wasn't even sure if Sebastian would want to hear from her. She almost cost him five million dollars! *The poor man*, she thought. Ever since she'd met him, she had been nothing but a plight on his life.

Lexi didn't know who else to call but she needed to talk to friends so she dialed her home in Atlanta.

"Hello."

"Dale! It's great to hear your voice," Lexi gushed.

"Lexi, is that you? Let me get Simone. Hang on...SI-MOOOOOONE!" he hollered. "Pick up the phone! It's Lexi!"

"Lexi! Oh my God! I've been watching the news and it's all about YOU! Are you okay?"

"Hi Simone. Yeah, somehow, I'm okay. How are you guys?"

"Who cares about us? Tell me all about what happened to you. Were you raped? I can barely even say those words. Did he beat you? Did–"

Lexi interrupted her. "Simone, I just wanted to let you know I'm fine. What's new at home? Did you get the carpets cleaned?"

"The carpets? They don't matter. You're the big news," Simone said excitedly.

"I've gotta go. It's good to hear both your voices. Bye." Lexi hung up the phone as fast as she could. She was tired of her life being a source of entertainment for Simone. She was quite upset that all Simone was interested in was the gory details. She didn't actually seem to care about Lexi, just gossip. Lexi longed to have a normal conversation. Should she call Greg? After the way they left things, that was probably a bad idea. She couldn't think of anyone else to call.

Lexi motioned to the officer that she was done with the phone. He took her into another room where she was given something to eat. While she dined on an adequate ham and cheese sandwich, a shrink asked her about her mental state. He wanted to know how she was coping with the trauma.

Lexi looked around and took note of the absurdity of the situation. First, she had gotten better food from the kidnapper. Second, the doctor kept asking her about how she felt. She'd only been free for a few hours. How could she possibly know how this event would affect her future mental condition? Shouldn't he know that?

Finally, the interrogation was over and Agent Young asked Lexi where she wanted to go.

"He's still on the loose, which means I'm still at risk, doesn't it?" she asked him in a moment of clarity. She felt afraid.

"Yes, I can see how you'd feel like you're not out of the woods until we have him, but these people usually don't come back. He's likely skipped town by now. We'll put out an all points bulletin on him using the details you provided, asking hospitals and eye doctors especially to be on the look out. Someone will see him. We WILL get him."

"But what do I do in the meantime? How do I stay safe? Should I go back to Atlanta?" she asked.

"Actually, we need you to stay here in town for a little while as we begin to round up suspects."

"Can I go to Sebastian Hawk's house?" she asked. "It's not like I want to meet a celebrity. We're friends, really," she explained.

"Yes, we know. We have your pocketbook and suitcase full of clothes that he gave us. I'll take you over there myself. Are you ready to go?" he asked.

Of course Lexi was ready to go. Police stations were terrible places to be. She saw all kinds of victims and criminals which, on their own, made the place uncomfortable for her. But to keep going over her personal story of abduction was extremely painful.

"Absolutely," she replied.

Agent Young drove Lexi to Sebastian's and he was actually looking forward to witnessing their reunion. This was a good part of his job, though it wasn't quite as rewarding to him as putting sociopaths behind bars.

When they arrived at Sebastian's there were several people outside his gate; Reporters, photographers and curious onlookers. Agent Young buzzed the gate.

"Yeah? What do you want?" Sebastian was tired of all the reporters pushing that buzzer.

"Mr. Hawk. It's Agent Young."

As they drove through the gate, Lexi became a little nervous. How would he react to seeing her, she wondered. She'd decided that if Sebastian didn't want her there, she would simply go to a hotel, but she'd hire Victor and Marcus to be her bodyguards.

Agent Young escorted Lexi to Sebastian's front door. Sebastian saw them walking towards the house through his security camera's monitor. He couldn't believe it was Lexi. The door flung open and he went running to her.

All of the reporters' cameras were filming and snapping away as Lexi and Sebastian embraced. Sebastian held on to Lexi with all his might until he realized he might be crushing her. He took her hand, looked deep into her eyes, and then led her into the house. Agent Young brought in her things and then left to go hunt down the kidnapper.

Matt, Wayne, and Sam were all in the house when Lexi arrived. They each greeted her and Sam gave her a huge hug. It was as warm of a welcome as she could have hoped for. Lexi felt as though these near strangers were her family.

The group of men soon left so Lexi and Sebastian could be alone. They went into the living room to talk. Sebastian's living room was fancy, but it was also cozy. It had a warmth about it that made people feel at ease. Lexi curled right up on the small sofa and Sebastian covered her with the multicolored throw blanket his mother had crocheted several years earlier.

Sebastian brought Lexi a hot cup of coffee and whatever leftovers he could find, mostly Thai food.

Lexi wasn't hungry, but Sebastian's parents had taught him that food was always a good way to comfort people.

"Sebastian, I'm so sorry for all of this," Lexi said.

"What do you mean YOU'RE sorry? It's my fault. I never should have let you go to that banquet alone."

"That's true," she joked. As she smiled, Sebastian's heart became full.

"It was a nice banquet," she continued, "aside from the stupidity on my part at the end."

"Really? What did you do there?" he asked, trying to follow her lead.

It was great how they could have a simple conversation about normal things like an awards banquet. Lexi was happy that Sebastian was sensitive enough to realize that grilling her about what she'd just been through might make her feel worse.

To keep her entertained, Sebastian regaled Lexi with stories of his crazy life. She couldn't believe how harshly Amanda had behaved. What a bitch! And when he told her about how his long drive with Gwen turned into an ill-advised 'raid date', they both chuckled.

"You ordered twelve different Chinese dishes? Are you insane? You could have fed the entire LA police force with all that food," she teased.

"Yeah, but I wouldn't share it with anyone except Gwen, my true beloved," he replied.

"I can't wait to get a dress for your wedding. Will it be a Spring affair or were you two thinking more in terms of June?"

It felt good to laugh, and great to laugh together.

"Do you want to get washed up and take a rest upstairs?" he offered.

"Yeah, I'm so tired and I have to get out of these clothes. He gave them to me."

As Lexi said those words and looked at what she was wearing, she felt a wave of anxiety sweep over her. She suddenly began to cry. Sebastian went to Lexi and held her tightly. He rocked her and then picked her up and carried her upstairs. Sebastian put Lexi down in his bathroom. He turned on the faucets of his huge whirlpool bathtub and went back downstairs to fetch her stuff.

Lexi bathed for half an hour and Sebastian stayed downstairs the entire time. He wanted to give her some space. He still had no idea what she'd been through, and he could only imagine the anguish she must have been feeling.

As Lexi soaked, Sebastian steamed. He was coming to terms with all of the anger the whole ordeal had created within him. Aside from living in fear for Lexi's safety, he couldn't stand to be made a fool of. How could he have been tricked by someone into thinking they were The Leech? It was a personal assault to his ego.

Sebastian knew that even though Lexi was safe

with him, she could never really relax until the kidnapper was found. Sebastian was going to catch him, he decided. He would be clever. He would be observant. He would make James Gilbert look like an amateur.

Chapter 24 – Him!

After close to an hour had passed, Sebastian went upstairs to check on Lexi. He knocked softly on his bedroom door and then opened it slowly. She was fast asleep, wrapped neatly in his covers. She looked so peaceful. He still didn't know if the bastard had laid a hand on her, and he was too afraid to ask. Sebastian considered sleeping in his guest room because he didn't want to upset Lexi in any way and he thought waking to a man's face might scare her. He stepped closer to admire her and she rolled over, opened her eyes and looked up at him sweetly.

"Are you going to join me?" Lexi asked.

"Do you want me to? I can sleep in another room if you prefer."

"Don't be stupid. This is your room," she told him in her usual blunt way. "Besides, I feel safe when you're around."

Sebastian liked that she considered him her protector. He felt manly. So, even though it was early, Sebastian got undressed and climbed under the covers too. He wrapped his long arms around her and watched Lexi as she slept. He enjoyed listening to the rhythm of her breath until he eventually closed his eyes and fell into a light sleep.

Sebastian awakened every hour or so to check on Lexi, but she was down for the long haul. At around 7:00 a.m., Lexi awoke, but by then Sebastian was finally enjoying a sound sleep. She went downstairs to fix herself some breakfast.

There wasn't much to eat in his house, other then the Thai food he tried to feed her the previous night. She grabbed a couple of eggs and some shredded cheese and whipped up an omelet for herself. Lexi would've made one for Sebastian too, but she didn't know how much longer he'd be asleep and cold omelets are just nasty. She figured she'd make him a hot meal when he got up.

Lexi enjoyed her omelet. She enjoyed her freedom. She roamed around Sebastian's home feeling completely comfortable. It was strange to think that they'd only spent a few days together, yet she felt such a strong connection to him. He was, in fact, her closest friend.

That thought made Lexi happy and also sad. How was it that she'd lived over a quarter of a century and had no one she considered a best friend? Sure, she had friends, but they were really

just her coworkers or people she knew who would
never become more than mere acquaintances.
Most of the women she met were fine to go to the
movies with, but they weren't the kind of people
who had any real interest in getting to know what
made Lexi tick. After some moments of reflection,
Lexi realized that when it came right down to it,
she was alone.

Was it something she had done on purpose?
Was she isolating herself from others because she
was afraid that when people found out about her
father's record or her problems with The Leech
they would reject her? Perhaps. Why was it so
easy to talk with Sebastian? He was so kind and
he seemed to have a genuine interest in her life, or
was he just *acting* polite? She wasn't sure what his
motives were, but she decided to take him at face
value. Besides, at that moment, there was no other
place she'd rather be.

Sebastian came downstairs wearing shorts and
a t-shirt. His hair was a mess and Lexi thought he
looked adorable.

"What smells so good?" he asked.

"I made myself some eggs. I hope you don't
mind. Do you want some? I make a mean cheese
omelet!"

"Sounds wonderful," he said.

As Lexi cooked, Sebastian put on a pot of
coffee. He watched her make her way around
his kitchen and it reminded him of his mother.
Amanda didn't cook any better than Sebastian,

which meant they were forever eating out. A home-cooked meal, even if it was only an omelet, was a big deal to Sebastian.

"This is great!" he complimented Lexi.

"Glad you like it," she smiled. She sat next to him at the kitchen table and watched him eat.

"What?" he asked.

"Nothing."

"Why are you looking at me like that? Do I have something stuck to my chin?" Sebastian grabbed a napkin and wiped it around his mouth. It got caught on his morning beard and left little pieces of paper on his face.

Lexi laughed. "*Now* you have something on your face – napkin lint!" She took her hand and wiped his face until all of the pieces were gone. "There, much better," she told him.

"What do you want to do today?" he asked.

"I don't know. Do you have any thoughts?"

"Well, I want to catch the bastard who took you, that's my mission," he said. "I'm so happy you're okay. You are okay, aren't you?"

"Yeah, I am," she responded.

"I was worried sick about you. Every moment of every day that you were gone, I was trying to find you."

"Really?" Lexi didn't know that Sebastian had devoted himself to rescuing her. She realized that he really did care for her.

"Absolutely. All I did day and night was try to figure out where you were so I could save you."

"Oh, Sebastian!" Lexi looked at him with her eyes wide. "I can't thank you enough. But I'm here and I'm okay, really. You can relax a little now."

"I can't relax until we get him," Sebastian told her.

"The FBI will get him," Lexi assured him.

"Like how they got you? Do you really think they can do it? I'm beginning to have my doubts. YOU, on the other hand, are ABSOLUTELY AMAZING! I've never met anyone like you."

"What do you mean, like *me*?" Lexi was concerned that Sebastian thought she was odd.

"You're smart. And honest. And beautiful. Is it okay if I kiss you?"

Lexi leaned into Sebastian and they kissed softly.

"You see, you're perfect!" he told her.

"No, not perfect, but close," she said in a smart-alecky way. "Did you know that my pinky toe has a tiny nail? So you see, not so perfect at all."

"Let me see that baby toe."

Lexi held up her foot and Sebastian lifted it closer to his face to inspect it. "Yeah, you're right. Ugly! A real deal breaker!"

Lexi pulled her foot away. "And what's wrong with you?" she asked. "Because you seem pretty damn perfect yourself, though you suck as a fake detective. I'd have been an old lady if I had to wait around for you to rescue me," she teased.

"That's my problem. Not very smart at all. But

some people find that being around a simpleton, such as myself, is a boost to their own ego. You would always seem brilliant if you were with me!"

"I'm already brilliant, you said so yourself," she told him.

"Yes, you are," he replied.

"Well, I think you're brilliant too," Lexi smiled. "I'm not buying that dumb-but-has-a-pretty-face routine for a minute. You're not a good enough actor to pull that off. You're smart and you're gonna have to own up to it."

"Yeah, if you insist."

Sebastian got up and carried his plate to the kitchen sink. Lexi watched him rinse it and put it into the dishwasher, just as she had done with hers.

"So, now what? We can't eat all day. Besides, you don't have any food here even if we wanted to," Lexi said.

"We could go to the grocery store. But they will follow us everywhere, you can count on that. You're a celebrity in your own right now, Lexi. They're calling your escape 'The Bus Breakout'. I wouldn't be surprised if they made a movie about you."

"Who do you think would play me?" she wanted to know.

"There isn't anyone who could portray you as far as I'm concerned. You're one of a kind!" he told her.

"Good answer."

"Let's get dressed and then we can talk about how to nail that son of a bitch, if that's okay with you?" Sebastian suggested.

"Yeah, his ass is grass, or whatever that saying is."

Sebastian laughed. "I don't think that's the best cliché for the occasion, but I know what you mean."

They went up to Sebastian's room to get cleaned up and dressed. As Lexi brushed her teeth, she spoke loudly to Sebastian who was in the bedroom.

"Did I tell you how I got away?"

"No, I don't know anything about what happened, but I'd love to know if you want to tell me."

Lexi spit the toothpaste out of her mouth. "I shoved teeth whitener into his eyes and then ran like hell!"

"Teeth whitener? What a *bright* idea!"

Lexi got the pun. "Ha, ha! Yeah, that stuff is meant to clean all the stains from your teeth so I figured it must have some strong chemicals in it that aren't very optically friendly."

"Actually, it's ingenious!" he told her.

"Thanks!" she replied.

"Lexi, I don't want to upset you, so tell me if this is crossing any lines, but did he force himself on you?" Sebastian asked delicately.

"Thank God, NO! He watched me shower, though, which I thought was weird as hell. And when I got out of the shower he grabbed my boobs once, but that was it. No other touching. Not even pushing or hitting or anything rough like that. He was a strange kidnapper. I'm guessing he wasn't a career criminal. He was mild-mannered, thankfully."

"I'm so relieved to hear it. Can I give you a hug?" Sebastian asked.

"You don't have to keep asking me, Sebastian. I know you're not a creep. Your touch feels good to me, really." She walked over to Sebastian and they hugged each other.

Sebastian began to stroke her hair and then kiss her neck. Lexi melted in his arms. It was such a loving moment for both of them. They kissed each other for a little while and then they finished getting dressed.

"I'm going to put some things into the laundry. Do you want me to take your bag and wash your stuff?" he asked.

Lexi was surprised and impressed that Sebastian did his own laundry. He was so different from what other people might have expected of a TV celebrity. He was just a regular guy. Well, a super-hot, super-kind, and super-rich regular guy, but a normal person nonetheless.

"My stuff needs to be washed on delicates. I'll come help you," she said.

When they were done putting the laundry in the machines, they headed towards the media room. Sebastian thought it would be fun if they

played some kind of board game and he had a
stack of them in the media room's closet. As he
surveyed the selection, Lexi continued to explore
the house. She went into Sebastian's office and
snooped around.

Suddenly, Sebastian heard Lexi's
blood-curdling scream,"AAAAAAAAAAHHHHH!!!!!!!!!
IT'S HIM! IT'S HIM!"

Sebastian ran to her. "Where? Where is he?"

Sebastian looked for something that he could
use as a weapon. There was a stapler but that
wouldn't do much harm. He picked up the silver-
plated letter opener he was given as a Christmas
gift by the president of his bank and asked, "Where
is he?"

Sebastian thought someone was in the house
or outside a window. What shocked him was when
Lexi just stood still and pointed to a picture on a
shelf in his bookcase.

"Who?" he asked looking at the picture.

"Him. That one!" she said with certainty.

"That's who took you?

"Yeah, that guy. Is he a friend of yours?" Lexi
looked at Sebastian quizzically.

"He used to be. Oh my God! I'm gonna beat the
shit out of him."

"We have to call Agent Young right away," Lexi
insisted.

"Hello, this is Sebastian Hawk," Sebastian said
when Agent Young answered his phone.

"Good morning Mr. Hawk. We are still working

on things if that's why you're calling."

"Actually, Lexi wants to tell you something."

"I know who he is!" Lexi said with excitement.

"Really? Who?" Agent Young asked.

"His name's Tom! He was Sebastian's assistant until Sebastian caught him with his girlfriend, Amanda, in St. Thomas. He must be trying to ruin Sebastian's life for some reason," she offered.

"Miss Lincoln, may I please speak with Mr. Hawk?"

"Sure." She handed the phone back to Sebastian.

"This is quite a development. What's his full name?" Agent Young asked. "Is his first name Tom or Thomas?"

"Tom Froughtly. He goes by Tom," Sebastian replied.

"How do you spell Froutly?"

"F-R-O-U-G-H-T-L-Y."

"He used to work for you?"

"Yes."

"So you can tell me his social security number and his contact information?"

"Absolutely!"

Sebastian proceeded to tell Agent Young everything he knew about Tom.

Sebastian was completely surprised by Lexi's finding. Tom had worked for Sebastian for three years and Sebastian had always treated him like a close friend. Sebastian couldn't understand why Tom would behave the way he did, first by cheating with Amanda, and then by kidnapping Lexi and demanding five million dollars from him. How could Tom turn out to be such a terrible person? He was with Sebastian practically every day. Why didn't Sebastian notice that there was something mentally off with that guy? Sebastian was beyond outraged. He visualized himself pummeling Tom to death, which made him feel better.

While the news was shocking, it was also somewhat comforting. At least now they knew who to look for. Sebastian e-mailed Agent Young the photo that Lexi used to ID Tom and it went out to police stations everywhere. The FBI would find his license plate and could post it on the big digital signs on the freeway so everyone would be looking for him. Tom was as good as found!

Chapter 25 – Manhunt

Lexi and Sebastian expected the phone to ring any minute with good news, however Agent Young never called. By ten o'clock that night, Sebastian began to feel frustrated.

"Lexi, I don't have a lot of faith in the FBI, as I told you earlier. I can't imagine what could be taking them so long! They know everything about Tom so he should be really easy to find."

"Actually, *you* know everything about Tom," Lexi told Sebastian.

"That's true. Okay, let me think for a minute. Where would he go? Oh my God! Do you think he's with Amanda?" There was a look of disbelief on Sebastian's face when he hypothesized about that.

"I don't know. Do you? Don't you think the FBI would go there first?" Lexi asked.

"Yeah, they should. To me, the idea of her being involved sounds crazy, but this whole thing is crazy," Sebastian said.

"Sebastian, did something happen between you and Tom or maybe between you and Amanda that would make them want to destroy you?"

"No. I don't think so. I wish I knew," he said. "I can't believe this is all because of me. What did I do that was so wrong to warrant their actions?"

"I'm not blaming you, and I don't think this is your fault at all," she explained. "I was just wondering out loud."

Sebastian felt bad. He thought this had to be his fault, in some unknown way.

"Let me pretend to be James for a few minutes," he said to Lexi.

"Okay. What would James do?" she asked.

"Yes, that's a good question."

Sebastian went into his office and began to look through his files and his own e-mails. That was Tom's territory. He took care of a lot of Sebastian's personal things.

As Sebastian searched through piles of papers and read endless e-mails, he came up with no useful information. Then, in a James-like moment of clarity, he thought to read his deleted e-mails.

"Lexi, look at this," he told her.

Lexi was sitting in his office reading a book she'd found in the house. She got up and stood next to Sebastian so she could see his computer. Sebastian pointed at the screen as he read the e-mail.

"It's from Tom's brother, Clark. He sent a few

e-mails to my account. It shows that I replied to him. But I've never even seen these before so of course I never replied. It had to be Tom, pretending to be me."

"Why did Clark write to you?"

"It says he wanted me to help Tom." Sebastian then read the e-mails aloud.

"Hello Mr. Hawk, I don't know if you're aware that Tom has been studying acting his whole life and he's extremely talented. He was cast in every school show since he was five. Yet, for some reason, my brother just can't seem to catch a break, but you've had such success. Do you think you could introduce him to the right people and help him get some acting jobs?"

"Did you know Tom wanted to be an actor?" Lexi asked.

"Yeah. I set up meetings for him with my agent and my manager. Unfortunately, they didn't think Tom had 'it' so they didn't sign him. But I believed in him and I was completely cool about him coming in late or leaving early on days when he had auditions."

"What did Tom write back to Clark, as you, I mean?"

"Clark, Tom's job is to take care of me and my career. If he wants to be an actor, then that's what he should do, rather than be my assistant. Even though I have been acting for just a few years and don't have as much talent as your brother, I've had a lot of good luck. You need to stop expecting me to

help him because it's not going to happen. Let him find his own good luck!"

"Wow, that's so harsh," Lexi said.

"Yeah, I would never say anything like that. I really did try to help him and he knows it."

"Did he go on a lot of auditions?" Lexi asked.

"Come to think of it, I can't remember the last time Tom went to a casting. Maybe he just got tired of the rejections and gave up on becoming an actor."

"That's probably it. I bet he didn't want his brother to be disappointed in him, you know, for giving up on his dream, so he chose to blame you for his failure."

"Here's a letter Clark sent in response to that one."

"Mr. Hawk, your unwillingness to recognize that Tom is largely responsible for your own good fortune is grotesque to me. You continue to hold him back, yet you would be nowhere if you didn't have Tom working for you. I hope you rot in hell you ungrateful, arrogant asshole!"

"Oh my God, it's so hostile and kind of scary!" she said. "It must have seemed to Clark like you were somehow standing in Tom's way, kind of sabotaging him."

"He thinks it's entirely my fault that Tom isn't a working actor." Sebastian's detective skills kicked in again. "Do you think Clark's involved in this with Tom? He threatened me in that e-mail."

"Yeah, now that you mention it, I think there's

a good chance that Clark has a part in all of this. What do you think we should do now?"

"Let's find out about Clark Froughtly."

Sebastian looked all over the Internet and only came up with a phone number and an address for Clark. He wasn't even sure if the information was current so he had thought about someone who could help him. Someone who had access to confidential files. In the morning, he would make the call.

He and Lexi went to sleep.

"Hello Sebastian. It's so nice to hear from you," Gwen said cheerily into the phone.

"Hi Gwen. How've you been? How are your adorable niece and nephew?"

"Wonderful. Thanks for asking. I understand that Miss Lincoln has found her way to safety. Congratulations! You must feel so relieved."

"Yes, I do. Thanks. But that's actually why I'm calling. I need your help."

"Oh? What can *I* do for you?"

"Agent Young is working very hard to find Tom Froughtly, the man Lexi identified as her kidnapper, so I don't want to disturb him. And I know you have a lot of important work that needs your attention, too. But...I was just wondering if you would take a few minutes and look up Clark Froughtly for me? It would mean a great deal to me if you would."

"I'm not at work now, but if you give me a few minutes, I can access some records from my home computer. His name is Clark Froughtly?"

"Yes. Thanks so much, Gwen. You're fantastic!" he encouraged her.

"Okay. Here he is."

"What does it say about him?" Sebastian asked.

"The most recent information we have shows that he's renting a place out by Big Bear. He was divorced five years ago and had his house foreclosed on six months ago. He has three kids, but his ex-wife has sole custody."

"Do you have an address for him?" Sebastian asked.

"Hang on, let me pull it up."

Gwen gave Sebastian the address to Clark's house, the name of his current employer and his phone numbers. She was extremely thorough.

"Is that all you need?" Gwen asked.

"You are beyond wonderful, Gwen. Did anyone ever tell you that?"

"I can never hear it enough!" she said playfully. "Do you want to get together sometime soon, Sebastian? Maybe we could have Chinese food again."

"It sounds great, but not for a little while. I'm sure you understand that right now, with Lexi's recent escape and all, there are a few other things I have on my plate. But definitely in the near future," he promised. And Sebastian meant it. He would be happy to take Gwen out to eat. She was a very nice lady who had been nothing but helpful to him. It was the least he could do.

Lexi listened to the whole exchange.

"I take back anything negative I've ever said about your acting talents. You are the master manipulator," she said while bowing to him.

"Let's not get carried away now, Lexi. All I did was get this guy's address. I'm sure you could have done the same, if Gwen was a man!"

"I don't know. You were pretty damn charming. I don't think I possess that level of bullshit. It's a gift," she told him.

"Ha! Thanks!"

Sebastian called Sam and asked him to come over. When Sam arrived, they told him about Clark and that they wanted to explore Clark's connection to Lexi's kidnapping."

"It does seem plausible," Sam agreed. "Shouldn't you call that FBI guy and let him follow up?"

"They'll just screw it up. Besides, if we're wrong, like I was with The Leech, I'll have wasted their time when they could've been out looking for Tom elsewhere."

"I get where you're coming from," Sam said. "What do you want to do?"

Sebastian turned to Lexi. "Would it be okay with you if I called the bodyguard people and had someone come to the house to hang with you while Sam and I go check this guy out?"

"Yeah, that's okay. But are you sure you should

go without the police? I don't want you to get hurt. Tom had a big knife that he threatened to cut me with. What if you actually do find him there with Clark and they come after you? Tom sounds like a desperate guy." Lexi was concerned for their safety.

"I've got a shotgun in my trunk," Sam volunteered.

They both looked at Sam in amazement. He seemed like such a pacifist. Sam saw their expressions and explained that he kept it there because on occasion he had to go into some very tough neighborhoods. The rule was the bigger the gun you have, the more likely you'll be left alone.

"Okay, then. We are armed and ready to go," Sebastian said.

"Sebastian, please promise me that you guys are just gonna check it out. If it looks like Tom's hiding out with Clark, then you'll call the cops, right? Please."

"Yes, of course. I promise."

Victor from Stealth Security was at Sebastian's house in about an hour, which gave Sebastian and Sam time to map out where Clark's place was and discuss what they'd do should they encounter Tom. Sebastian was very pumped up about the whole idea of finding Tom. He couldn't wait to get his hands on him and release his rage.

It took a little less than two hours for Sam to get them to Big Bear. Once they were in the area, they had to find the exact address that Gwen had provided. They drove up several windy hills which took them into the woods and eventually they turned down a dirt road where they came across a small cabin. That had to be it, they concluded.

The fact that it was so far from town made Sam a little nervous. What had he gotten himself into, he wondered. He never knew Sebastian to be reckless, but he feared that the whole situation might have just put Sebastian over the top.

"Sebastian, are you sure you don't want to call the police? This place is pretty remote," Sam advised.

"Let's just look around. I have my cell phone and you have your gun if we need it, so I think we'll be okay, don't you?"

"I hope so."

Sam parked the car up the hill from the house and then they carefully walked around to the back of the cabin. It was quiet. Perhaps no one was home. As they peered through a window, Sebastian thought he saw something move.

"Sam!" he whispered as he motioned for him to duck. They squatted so they couldn't be seen and then they slowly inched their eyes over the windowsill once again to see inside.

This time, Sebastian definitely saw someone walking across the room, but he wasn't sure if it was Tom. He needed a clearer view, so he and Sam quietly crept over to another window and looked in. All they saw from there was a table with a pile of papers on top of it. Sebastian tried to read what they said, but he couldn't make it out. Then Sam pointed at something.

"Over there. Do you see it?" Sam asked quietly.

"What? Where?"

"On that chair." Sam pointed.

Sebastian raised his head up a bit higher and saw a large knife with a towel next to it on top of a wooden chair.

"That must be the knife that son of a bitch used to threaten Lexi," Sebastian said.

They heard footsteps approaching and they quickly ducked down and listened. But the person inside didn't say anything. After a few minutes, they decided to check out another window. As they were walking towards a different vantage point, they heard a car approaching.

"Who's that?" Sam asked.

Sebastian motioned for Sam to follow him. They trotted bent over as fast as they could to the back of some shrubbery, which provided them with good camouflage and a view of the driveway. Through the leaves they watched as a black car, that looked like Sam's, stopped in front of the cabin. A man got out.

"There he is!" Sebastian said as he began to stand upright. Sam pulled him back down.

"Don't!" Sam insisted.

"I HAVE TO!" Sebastian told him.

Sebastian's adrenaline was pumping and, just as he was about to jump out from behind the bushes and attack Tom, the front door to the cabin flung open.

"Hey. Did you get the burgers?" he heard a male voice ask.

"Yeah," Tom said as he went inside.

Sebastian was fuming. He missed his opportunity.

"Sam, let's go to the car and get your shotgun," Sebastian instructed.

They walked to the car and Sam convinced Sebastian to get in so they could drive farther down the road and talk. Sam stopped about a mile away from the cabin.

"What?" Sebastian asked. "What do you want to say?"

"I think it's time to call the police," Sam said reasonably.

"But we can take them, Sam. They only have a knife and you have a big gun. Rock, paper, scissors, man – gun trumps knife!" Sebastian explained his reasoning.

"What if they have a gun, too?"

"I'm not afraid of Tom. I know that guy. He's not so tough," Sebastian insisted.

"Let's go get the cops," Sam said. "Isn't that what James would do in a situation like this? Isn't that the smart move?"

Sam was rational and, even though he wanted to, Sebastian couldn't argue. He knew his character/alter ego, Detective James Gilbert, would have allowed the police to capture the perpetrators once he'd solved the crime.

"Okay, fine. But we could've taken them," Sebastian insisted.

"Yes, I'm sure you're right," Sam agreed.

They drove into town and, with the help of Sam's GPS, located the Big Bear police station. When they went in, the first thing they noticed was the mellow atmosphere. It was a tremendous contrast from the frenzied police departments in LA. Yes, they were definitely in the mountains.

Sebastian walked up to the counter and spoke to a young man who escorted them through a door and then into a small room. "Officer Neshman will be with you gentlemen shortly," he told them.

Officer Neshman was about the same age as Sam, somewhere in his late forties. He heard what the men had to say and then called Agent Young from the FBI, using the number that Sebastian provided.

"Agent Young said you should wait here for him," Office Neshman told the men.

"No way! I'm not sitting here for two hours while that lunatic Tom is free to leave." Sebastian stood up. "You guys have to go get him or WE will," he threatened.

Officer Neshman called Agent Young back and told him what Sebastian said. He then put Sebastian on the phone with Agent Young so they could speak directly to each other.

Sebastian pled his case and then, when he was finally satisfied with the answer, handed the phone back to Officer Neshman.

"Yes. Yes. All right. I will tell the others. Thank you." Officer Neshman then hung up.

Sebastian was sitting on the edge of the table when the officer addressed him and Sam. "Okay, so there's an FBI agent who's not far from here. He should be here shortly. He'll meet with my boss to arrange Mr. Froughtly's capture. May I get you gentlemen something to drink while we wait?"

"Maybe we should go into town and have a bite to eat, Sam," Sebastian suggested.

"I don't think that's a good idea, Mr. Hawk. People will recognize you and then word will spread. It's a small community here. If the suspect gets wind of your presence in town, he may flee," Agent Neshman advised.

"Yeah. Okay. Can we at least order some food to be delivered here? I'm hungry," Sebastian told him.

"Mary has the menus. She's the lady in the cubicle when you first came in. Just go ask her and I'm sure she'll be happy to help you order something to eat."

Mary? Sebastian thought. He couldn't get over the coincidence of the name and his thoughts returned to Lexi.

Chapter 26 – Heroes

Agent Collins had the opposite demeanor of Agent Young. He was lighthearted and jovial and once he entered the Big Bear police station the energy of the office changed...to fun. People were laughing and smiling, which made Sebastian angry. This was not the time for fun. This was the time for seriousness. What Tom had done to Lexi was very serious, not to mention what he'd done to Sebastian.

Sebastian, Sam, Agent Collins, and Police Chief Garrett all met in the conference room to discuss the situation. They didn't know if Clark was in the cabin with Tom or if someone else was involved. They would have to be very careful with how they made their approach.

After devising a plan of attack, the men and several additional officers all got into cars and headed to the secluded cabin. Just as Sebastian had witnessed before with the raid on The Leech, the men surrounded the building before announcing themselves. But this time things went down very differently.

"OPEN THE DOOR! FBI!" Agent Collins announced loudly. But the door didn't open, so he yelled it again. Then he shouted, "Come out, Mr. Froughtly, we have the place surrounded!" But the door still didn't open.

Was he gone? Sebastian wondered. He knew he and Sam should have just gotten Tom when they were there earlier. *Damn it!*

Bam! A couple of officers shoved a heavy battering ram into the door pushing it wide open. Many men charged inside with their weapons drawn.

Sebastian and Sam were outside, waiting safely behind a car. They could hear everything because the woods were so quiet.

"Get down, NOW!" one of the policemen shouted. "Put your hands on top of your heads. DO IT!"

And it was over, that fast. The police came out with Tom and presumably Clark in handcuffs. Sebastian thought he would feel happy to see Tom being taken away, but instead he had conflicting feelings. After all, up until a short while ago, Tom had been his close friend. Seeing him in handcuffs, looking like the criminal he was, was somewhat hard for Sebastian to come to terms with. Yet Sebastian still had a strong urge to kick the crap out of him.

Sebastian approached Tom. "You son of a bitch! How could you? After everything I did for you? I hope you're in jail for the rest of your pathetic life!"

As an officer put Tom into his squad car, Tom answered back. "You're the one with the pathetic life. You think being an actor makes you special? You're not so special. I know you, Sebastian. You're a fraud! You're not worth a dime, let alone the millions you make with your terrible acting!"

"Oh, I'm the fraud?" Sebastian said in disgust.

The officer closed the car door. The conversation between Tom and Sebastian would have to be continued another time, if ever at all.

Agent Collins came over to Sebastian. "Mr. Hawk, thank you for helping us find this asshole. Your assistance has been invaluable. By the way, I love your show and you're great on it. Don't let that loser make you think otherwise. You were just like Detective Gilbert today. Very impressive, really! When this is all done, do you think I could get your autograph?"

"Thanks, Agent Collins. That's nice of you to say. Of course," Sebastian replied. "So what's going to happen now?"

"They have to be taken to be booked. It's a lot of paperwork. Tomorrow you and Ms. Lincoln should meet with Agent Young. He'll take over everything from here. Again, thanks!"

"Should Sam and I just go home?" Sebastian asked.

"Yes."

"Okay. And thank YOU, Agent Collins. You and the guys were awesome."

Sebastian called Lexi from the car while he and Sam headed back to LA. She was ecstatic, of course. He told her that she should take Victor and go shopping to pick up something new to wear because tonight they were going out to celebrate!

"Why do I still need Victor if Tom's in jail?" she asked.

"The press will be all over you. Tell Victor it's his job to keep them at bay. Also, Victor can drive you. You don't know your way around."

"That's true. Where should I go to shop?" she wanted to know.

"Maybe the Beverly Center? They have everything there," Sebastian suggested.

"Okay. Great. I'm so excited! Finally, some fun!" Lexi said happily. Before she hung up she added, "Oh, and nice job, my handsome hero!"

Sebastian could imagine Lexi's smile as he spoke with her. It sounded like a big one that showed her dimple. He couldn't wait to get to her. Unfortunately, because of notorious LA traffic, the drive home took almost twice as long as the drive to Big Bear. He passed some of the time by calling Matt and debriefing him on what had happened.

Matt was thrilled by the news. He would get to tell the world that Sebastian Hawk was as brilliant in real life as the character he plays on TV. This was a very exciting moment for Matt, who'd been busy recently trying to counteract the abundance of bad press that Amanda's people had generated. Finally he got to throw a publicity parade for Sebastian Hawk!

When Sebastian reached home Lexi was already back from her shopping trip. As soon as he and Sam walked through the door Lexi ran into Sebastian's arms while gushing, "My heroes!" Sam wanted to leave them alone for the evening, but Sebastian and Lexi insisted he join in the celebration. Sam was a hero too. It was agreed that Sam would go to his house to change and then meet them at the restaurant later for dinner. Victor was no longer needed, so he was dismissed.

After Sam left, Lexi asked Sebastian to tell her everything that happened. He did. She was a little surprised by how brave he and Sam were to walk up to the cabin in the middle of the forest by themselves. She didn't think that was the smartest move, but it all worked out so she didn't say anything about it.

Sebastian took a shower and got dressed in the bathroom while Lexi put on her new outfit in the bedroom. She wore a short, lavender shift dress that loosely hugged her body in the right places. It was accessorized with strappy black heels and silver drop earrings. Even though Lexi couldn't decide on a hair color, her fashion sense was defined. She preferred demure dresses that merely hinted at her considerable assets. Her classy style was a far cry from the stripper look that was the current trend with women her age. But, as Sebastian discovered when he'd searched through her suitcase, Lexi liked tantalizing, provocative underthings.

"I'm mesmerized by you," Sebastian told Lexi when he saw her in her dress.

Lexi smiled a dimple smile and Sebastian couldn't take his eyes off her. She loved how he looked at her with such adoration. She thought he was pretty wonderful, too.

Lexi walked over to Sebastian and they began kissing. Passion overcame them both. They made their way to the bed, still lip locked. As they lay across his gray silk comforter, Sebastian's right hand sensually stroked Lexi's left arm, while his other hand made its way up her thigh. Lexi fumbled as she attempted to unbutton Sebastian's shirt. He removed his hands from Lexi's body to assist her with his buttons. It was that brief moment of pause that gave Lexi the time to reconsider.

"Sebastian, we're going to be late. I feel bad about leaving Sam at the restaurant, don't you?"

Sebastian didn't give a damn about Sam at that moment, but Lexi stood up and started to fix her hair. "Come on, we'll have plenty of time to celebrate privately later, I promise," she told him.

Sebastian didn't want to go to dinner. He wanted to spend the night making love to Lexi. His testosterone was pulsing through his veins. He grabbed Lexi's arm and pulled her back onto the bed. She didn't resist.

Sebastian couldn't wait to discover what frilly treats awaited him beneath Lexi's outfit. He acted quickly, unzipping her dress in one motion and then swiftly pulling it down to the floor. Ah, yes! Sheer black lace. He was excited by the reveal. Lexi kicked off her high heels while Sebastian peeled off his shirt and practically jumped out of his pants.

They were wild and reckless and body parts were thrashing about with great speed. Pillows plunged to the floor. Blankets were tossed aside in a frenzy. Noises of delight and gasps for air followed. They rolled. They twisted. They connected in the most intimate way two people can. And then, with one final thrust of passion – ecstasy!

They caught their breaths and enjoyed being still, together. Neither wanted to ruin the mood by speaking, but the fact still remained that time was passing and Sam was at the restaurant awaiting their arrival.

"Do you really want to go out?" Sebastian asked Lexi. "I can call Sam and cancel. I'm sure he'll understand."

Lexi kissed Sebastian. Their kisses became deeper and deeper and once again Sebastian became aroused. Lexi eagerly climbed on top of him, grabbing his hands in hers and squeezing

them securely as she rocked back and forth.
Sebastian pulled away for a breath and then
returned his lips to hers. She released his hands
and he reached for her breasts. At first he grabbed
them firmly, feeling his way around her particular
curves. Then he tenderly, and with an expert's
finesse, caressed her nipples until Lexi let out
several shrieks of pleasure. She collapsed onto
his chest. Sebastian squeezed her tightly, then
rolled Lexi over and took control. She held onto his
back as he moved steadily and forcefully until he,
too, was overcome by a warm rush of sensations.
Sebastian moaned in satisfaction.

They were sweaty, happy, and serene. But
Sebastian knew he had to contact Sam. Eventually,
he made himself get up to get his cell phone. He
sent Sam a text. "*Sorry. We're not coming. Charge
your dinner to me. Again, sorry.*"

It was a pretty shitty thing to do, but Sam
wasn't very surprised. He had seen how they
looked at each other and knew there was a good
chance he would be dining alone.

With daybreak came the nonstop phone calls from
the press. "Was it true that Sebastian captured the
kidnappers? Did he get shot in the process? Were
there really four of them?" The reports got more
and more outrageous. Then, when the names of
the suspects were released, an even bigger hysteria
began. "Was that really the same Tom who had

the affair with Amanda Evans? Was she part of his maniacal scheme? Did Sebastian mistreat his assistant so badly that he left him no choice but to resort to criminal behavior?"

Thank goodness Matt was the one who had to answer the inquiries. All Sebastian did was say "no comment." Matt released several statements on Sebastian's behalf throughout the day as things continued to unfold.

Lexi and Sebastian met with Agent Young in his office at around 10:00 a.m. They held hands as they sat side by side in the chairs in front of his desk. Agent Young told Lexi that she would have to identify Tom in a lineup later in the day. She was ready and willing to do so.

Sebastian had many questions for Agent Young. "What was Clark's involvement in the kidnapping?"

"We're not sure if he was involved at all," Agent Young told them. "Right now they're both denying that Clark did anything other than abet his brother by housing him after Miss Lincoln's escape."

Sebastian told Agent Young about Clark's e-mails to Sebastian that Tom had answered. Sebastian handed the printouts to Agent Young and asked, "Are these helpful?"

Agent Young read the letters and said, "Thank you. I'll put these in the file, but they don't directly implicate Clark in the crime. However they do help provide a motive for Tom."

"Yeah, let's talk about him for a minute,"

Sebastian said. "I realize that you do this all the time, but I don't get how someone can be my assistant, my friend, one minute and then betray me with Amanda, kidnap Lexi, and demand five million dollars from me the next. Is he mentally insane or something?"

"I can't speak for his mental state, Mr. Hawk. All I can tell you is that many crimes are committed because of jealousy. They happen every day, just not usually to this extent," Agent Young explained.

"Did Amanda have anything to do with this? Are they a team?" Sebastian didn't want to ask because he was afraid of the answer, but he knew he had to.

"We've interviewed Miss Evans and she claims that she was only with Mr. Froughtly that one time in St. Thomas. She said she was just using him as a plaything for her vacation and she had no other involvement with him beyond that. What do you think, Mr. Hawk?"

"Yeah, from what I've come to know about Amanda recently, that seems about right. I can't believe she would do anything criminal because it would hurt her precious career," Sebastian said.

"There is no evidence to indicate that Miss Evans had an ongoing relationship with Mr. Froughtly, if that's any consolation. However, we did find out that Miss Evans was the link between Mr. Froughtly and Mr. Orrington," Agent Young informed them.

"What do you mean? Amanda knows The Leech?"

"No. It seems that you discussed over the phone with Miss Evans the problems that Miss Lincoln was having with Mr. Orrington. Miss Evans told me that as soon as she hung up from speaking with you, Mr. Froughtly called her. She then proceeded to recount the information to him before telling him that she wasn't interested in seeing him again socially."

"Socially, is that what she called it?" Sebastian was pissed. "So what you're saying is that this IS my fault. Me and my big mouth? If I hadn't told Amanda about The Leech's calls, she wouldn't have told Tom, who then used that information to concoct a plan to impersonate The Leech and kidnap Lexi for ransom."

"You can't blame yourself, Mr. Hawk. You are not responsible for Miss Evans' or Mr. Froughtly's behaviors. It was her decision to gossip to him and his decision to break the law," Agent Young tried to console Sebastian.

Lexi looked at Sebastian and said, "Don't be silly. THIS IS SO NOT YOUR FAULT! You're my hero, my protector! And YOU found Tom! Plus, don't forget that right away you jumped into action to protect me from The Leech!" She put her arms around him. "Sebastian, you're awesome!"

Then Lexi turned to look at Agent Young, "Hey, Mr. Young, what's up with Travis anyway? Of course he wasn't the one who kidnapped me, but do you think someday he might?"

"We received word that after our raid, Mr. Orrington checked himself back into Rolling Pines. Some of the symptoms he experiences with his disorder are paranoid tendencies, which for him include a concern that the government is after him. Because the FBI showed up at his house demanding answers, his suspicions and fears were confirmed. I doubt he'll want to leave the safety of Rolling Pines ever again, which should make you feel safe too, Miss Lincoln. Besides, I honestly don't think Mr. Orrington has the capacity for kidnapping, from what I assessed when I met with him."

"That's great!" Lexi exclaimed. "I feel so free."

"You can go back to being Mary again if you want," Sebastian told her.

"Nah, I think Lexi's who I really am."

"I agree," Sebastian told her.

Later that day Sebastian took Lexi to the police station so she could review the lineup of suspects. Sebastian stood with her behind the two-way glass. Of course, he knew which guy Tom was, but he was not allowed to speak. Without any hesitation, Lexi pointed directly at Tom and said, "That's him." Clark participated in the lineup too, but other than having a slight resemblance to Tom, she didn't recognize him.

Lexi and Sebastian returned home to find Matt

waiting for them outside the gate.

Chapter 27 – Together?

"So you think if we go on *24-Hour Hollywood* together it will somehow be good for both of us?" Lexi asked Matt.

"Yes. Lexi, your story is too good for them to leave you alone without getting the dirt, and Sebastian's fans need to know that he's a real life hero."

"Matt, I don't mind doing the press stuff because it's part of my job, it's the life I chose. But Lexi can go back to Atlanta and this will all be yesterday's news, don't you think?"

"You want me to go back to Atlanta?" Lexi turned to look at Sebastian. She was shocked by his statement.

"No, I don't want you to go back to Atlanta, that's not what I said. I was just asking Matt a question."

"It sounded like you want me to leave. I can

leave if that's what you really want," Lexi said strongly.

"For the second time, I don't want you to leave," he insisted.

"Look guys. Don't get into a fight. That doesn't help anyone. All I'm suggesting is that if Lexi tells the media what they want to know, then they'll leave her alone," Matt explained.

"Matt, that's not how it works and you know it. The press and the gossip world have insatiable appetites. If Lexi decides to do it, she has to know that it doesn't guarantee they will leave her alone. It might simply stir the pot and lead to more interviews."

"You don't think I can handle interviews?" she asked Sebastian.

"Why do you keep twisting my words?"

Sebastian got up and stormed out of the room. He was so frustrated by the conversation.

Lexi looked at Matt. "Is this what he's normally like?"

Matt didn't know what to say so, for a change, he said nothing. He just shrugged his shoulders.

Lexi went looking for Sebastian. She found him in the media room with the TV on.

"You're watching TV? Really? Now?"

"Yes, it's a good game. I'm obviously not helping matters in there so I'm taking a break."

Lexi sat down next to Sebastian. He was behaving like a child so she thought she would talk to him as such. She stroked his hair and said,

"Sebastian. I know this has been a terrible day. You must have a lot of feelings about seeing Tom at the police station. I know I do. We don't have to talk to Matt about the media stuff now. I'm going to send him home, okay?"

Sebastian kept his eyes focused on the TV but he heard every word she said. "Okay," he replied.

After Matt left, Lexi felt out of place in Sebastian's house for the first time. She didn't know what to do so she went back into the media room and sat next to Sebastian while he watched a hockey game. When the second period of the game came to an end, he turned to Lexi and apologized.

"I'm sorry. I'm acting like a dick and I know it. I just don't know why. Maybe it's because the two people I thought cared about me the most, Amanda and Tom, didn't care about me at all. They actually hated me," he said with a sad expression. "I guess I'm just afraid that you're going leave me too."

Lexi knew what it was like to feel alone. That's how she felt when she had no one to call from the police station after her escape. It was a terrible feeling. She put her arms around Sebastian, but didn't say a word.

They stayed cuddled through the entire third period of the hockey game and, except for the occasional shouting at the players on TV, they didn't talk. They simply gelled.

When the game was over they had a real talk.

"What do you want to do, Lexi, do you know?" Sebastian asked.

"Sebastian, I have no idea, but I don't want to abandon you."

"So this is a pity thing?"

"Yeah, exactly. Poor gorgeous, smart, successful Sebastian Hawk, who has women chasing him down streets. I do pity you. How can you manage without me?" she said.

"What do you mean? Are you being sarcastic? I can't tell."

"I mean, I'm the one who's insecure here, dummy," she said. "I'm just a dental hygienist who ruined your life. Why do you want to keep me around? You're a famous actor who's kind, talented, smart, handsome, and can have any woman he wants. I'm the one who's all alone. You were there when Greg walked out on me. I have no one who cares about me either, you know."

"First of all, you are not JUST anything. You are Lexi Lincoln, the most spectacular woman I've ever met. You're beautiful, smart, and wonderfully real, with a warm smile and a tiny toenail!" he told her. "The truth is, I'm afraid you're going to figure out that you're far too good for me, a fake detective. No one wants to be with me, really. They just want James Gilbert, like Greg did. And I might as well fess up about Greg. I saw an e-mail he sent you. Even that asshole knows a good thing when he sees it. He apologized. So if you want to leave me for him, then I guess there's nothing I can do about it."

"Greg apologized?"

"Really? That's all you heard me say?" Sebastian got up in a huff and started to walk out of the room.

"Sebastian," Lexi raised her voice. "You can't just walk away every time I say something you don't like. Come back here and talk to me."

Sebastian hated the way she had spoken to him. He didn't want to be told what to do by anyone, but he knew his actions were fueled by a lot of emotions that he was having trouble controlling. He stopped and turned around to look at Lexi. Her face was so sweet. He walked back to where she was and sat down.

"Thank you," she said.

"This probably isn't the best time to talk to me," he admitted. "Both of us have been through a lot in the last few days so maybe we should just process our feelings and then we can talk later," Sebastian suggested.

"Yes, we've BOTH been through a lot that we HAD to face on our own. But now we can help each other. Don't push me away. I see what you're doing."

He looked at her. How come she was so wise?

"Okay. So what should we talk about? How much we're both hurting? How neither of us wants to be alone? How we don't know where to go from here?" Sebastian asked sincerely.

"Yes."

"You start," he told her.

"Fine. The truth is, I don't know what to do.

Should I go back to Atlanta and pretend this never happened? Even if I wanted to, and I'm not saying I do, I don't think that's an option. My mom said I was on CNN! CNN's based in Atlanta. All of my patients will know what happened to me and so will everyone I meet there, wherever I go."

"They'll all know it here, too," Sebastian said.

"Yeah, but here I have a good friend – YOU."

Sebastian looked at Lexi. She was once again honest and open with him, which was something he'd admired from the very first time they met... the moment he unknowingly had fallen in love with her.

"Yes, *here you have me*. I guess the real question is, do you WANT me? And I don't mean it to sound like that, but you know what I mean."

Lexi looked at Sebastian. It was a straightforward question that required a straightforward answer. She listened to her heart.

"Yes," she said assuredly. "I want you."

Sebastian smiled. The tension in the room started to lift. He reached over and held her hand.

With a tad of hesitation, she in turn asked him, "Do you want *me*?"

"Without a doubt!" he told her.

"Okay then," she said, snuggling into his chest.

"Okay then," he replied.

– The End –

**Look for other books by Brandy Cohen
including The Perfect Recipe -
*a delicious love story told through texts,
emails and social media:***

The Perfect Recipe

A DELIGHTFUL, FAST-PACED NOVEL ABOUT
SELF-DISCOVERY, FAMILY RELATIONSHIPS AND
CRAZY, HOT LOVE.

No one expects Franki Jacobs to have a meteoric
rise to fame and fortune, least of all, Franki
Jacobs. But, after several years of personal and
professional struggles, 28-year-old Franki makes
a bold move to Ft. Lauderdale in search of
happiness. There she begins a new job working
for the handsome and mysterious Big Ben, setting
into motion a series of events that changes both
of their lives in ways neither could have imagined.
With relatable characters, clever dialogue and
unexpected plot twists, Cohen creates the perfect
recipe for a truly irresistible story.

Available at www.BrandyCohen.com
ISBN 978-0-578-09045-0

Contact Brandy Cohen:
brandy@brandycohen.com
www.brandycohen.com
www.facebook.com/catalystbooks
Your kind comments and feedback are welcomed.

....

If you would like to improve your life through
personal life coaching, please send an e-mail to
info@ahappierlife.com.

....

To arrange an appearance or book signing by
Brandy Cohen, please e-mail info@catalystbooks.

Made in the USA
Middletown, DE
18 April 2015